THE MIDNIGHT WISH

RITE WORLD: LIGHTGROVE WITCHES

JULIANA HAYGERT

RITE WORLD

Welcome to the RITE WORLD!

For a printable reading order, click here!

Free Novellas:
The Vampire Hunt
The Light Witch

Novellas:
The Hunter Path
The Light Calling
The Light Witch
The Wicked Alliance
The Shadow Fae

And more to come!

AUTHOR'S NOTE

I hope you enjoy reading *The Midnight Wish*!

Don't forget to sign up for my Newsletter to find out about new releases, cover reveals, giveaways, and more!

If you want to see exclusive teasers, help me decide on covers, read excerpts, talk about books, etc, join my reader group on Facebook: Juliana's Club!

1

I stepped into my bedroom and looked around—it had only been a couple of weeks since we were here last, and yet it felt like an eternity.

After recovering the necklace, the grimoire, and bringing Sean back to himself, we left Europe in haste, afraid that more Brotherhood of Purity members or dark witches would find us again.

On the flight back to the United States, the sisters bought us all first-class tickets. I hated those because they were all separate and I couldn't hold Sean's hand or talk to him without a narrow corridor between us.

However, I wasn't sure if Sean would have spoken to me, even if he could. He barely looked at me.

"What's wrong?" I had asked, worried he was in pain or a remnant of the darkness remained inside of him.

"Nothing," he had said quickly. "It's just ... my head hurts and my thoughts are confusing." Then he had marched out of the crumbling house and avoided being near me.

The only time he interacted with us was while waiting in the customs line at the airport. The sisters were discussing where we should hide, and Sean mentioned the house where they told us we were Arianna and Thales.

"But what about the Darkmist?" Anna asked. "Don't they know about that place?"

Sean shook his head. "I didn't tell them or anyone else."

That was surprising but welcome. That house was the perfect hiding place, and since it hadn't been compromised, we didn't hesitate.

I dropped my duffel bag on my bed—we had stopped at the inn in Terentia to pick up our things—and turned to the door as Sean walked by. He had stayed in this room with me, but apparently, that was done. He asked the sisters for one of the other empty suites. Of course, they didn't object, but I was sure they were wondering the same thing I was: What the hell was going on?

Tired of this shit, I marched into the corridor and saw Sean stopped in front of the last door, the farthest from mine. The window beside the door shone a dark gold as the sun started to set, creating a gilded halo around Sean.

For a moment, I stared at him, in awe of his beauty. Tall with broad shoulders, hard muscles in all the right places. And his face ... puckered lips, sharp chin and jaw, and his bright blue eyes contrasted well with his fair skin and his chestnut brown hair. The sides weren't as short as before, but the top was still longer.

I shook myself and put my hands on my waist. "Are you going to ignore me?" Between traveling and whatnot, it had been almost two days since he was back to himself ... two entire days that he had avoided me.

Sean let out a long sigh but didn't turn to me. "Drop it, Hazel. I'm not in the mood to talk."

"What happened? You woke up, remembered who you are, who you were before, and suddenly you don't love me anymore? I disgust you?"

He faced me, his eyes hard. "I disgust myself. I should disgust *you*. All the things I've done ... it's everything in here." He tapped his forehead. "And here." Then his heart. "I can't erase it; I can't forget it. I still feel it ... all that anger, all that rage. The hunger for power, for death. I remember all the people I killed and how it didn't faze me at all." He winced. "I don't have a choice but to be here, but right now, I want to be left alone."

He entered the bedroom and slammed the door shut.

I stayed frozen in place for a moment, whiplashed from his words. No, this wasn't how our story went. He was supposed to be at my side, helping me, and fighting all the evil beings with me. I took a step forward, determined to talk to him, but a firm hand on my shoulder stopped me.

I turned.

Shade squeezed my shoulder gently. "He needs time, Hazel."

"Well, we don't have time," I snapped.

"Think about how you felt after killing that witch to save him. Now increase that tenfold. Who knows, maybe ever more? And you did it to save someone you love. Some of his killings were for pure enjoyment. That has to take a toll."

My shoulders sank. By the light, I had almost drowned in sorrow after killing that witch. I couldn't imagine doing it repeatedly. And he remembered it all. I shuddered. Jeez, that couldn't be easy.

"I hadn't thought about that." And now I felt bad. How selfish of me. All I had thought so far was that he was the love of my life, and I was supposed to be his, and he was ignoring me.

"Come on." Shade took my hands in his. "I'll make you some tea."

Numb, I let Shade guide me downstairs to the kitchen. He helped me sit on one of the chairs around the kitchen table while he went to the pantry and grabbed whatever he needed to make the tea.

Holy shit, I hadn't put myself in Sean's shoes yet. I had been so focused on getting the items, getting him back, getting the hell out of there, I hadn't considered anything else.

Was I a bitch, or what?

I to be there for him. To comfort him, to support him, to hug him. I wanted him to know I loved him no matter what, and that I would be here for him forever.

Shade put a mug in front of me, then he sat down across from the table with a mug for himself.

"I know what you're thinking," he said. "Don't. I meant it. He needs time."

"He sure does," Anna said as she entered the kitchen.

Britta was right behind her. They went to the range, grabbed the kettle, and prepared tea for themselves.

With their mugs in hand, they sat with Shade and me around the table.

I glanced at my phone. It was six in the evening, and we were having tea. My stomach was growling, but I didn't have the energy to make dinner.

Sean was probably hungry too, right? I should make dinner for him. I glanced at the fridge and started getting up.

"If you're worried about dinner, I've got it covered," Shade said.

Frowning, I sat back down. It was weird knowing about his connection to me and now feeling it. He couldn't tell my exact thoughts, but he certainly could guess what they were about, what feelings were associated to them.

"How?" I asked.

"I've ordered takeout. In about fifteen minutes, I'm going to pick it up."

"Good," Britta said. "I'm hungry."

"We all are," Anna stated. "Hungry and tired. We should go to bed after dinner, and sleep until noon tomorrow. The light knows we need the rest."

"But we've got a lot to do," I said, my voice low.

Anna nodded. "Yes, we do. But we can't do anything if we're barely standing. First, we rest. Then, we act."

I took a sip of my tea. I would act in two fronts: our main, joint mission, and also with Sean. Somehow, in some way, I would help him, and he would feel whole again. It wouldn't happen overnight, but I was sure that with time and love, he would overcome his demons.

I set my mug down. "So, what's the plan now? Storm the Light Castle and get my ashes? And then what?"

"First we need to assess the situation," Britta said. "Grace caused trouble and framed you, and the Light Order is searching for you."

I picked up my phone. "I know someone I trust. I'll ask her to meet me, and she can tell us what's going on."

Anna's brows knotted. "Who do you trust?"

"Sadie," I said, positive Sadie wouldn't betray me, even if she didn't agree with me. "I'll text her."

"Speaking of texting." Britta held up her phone. A moment later, she looked at me. "They will arrive tomorrow around noon."

A mix of relief and apprehension coursed through me. During the trip back, Britta and Anna talked to their friend who was taking care of my mother and sister. I didn't like the idea of keeping them spelled while this mess was going on, and who knew how long it would take? So, I asked them if my mother and sister could be brought to us. I would explain everything, and hopefully, they would understand. If they didn't, then I would spell them to keep them locked inside the house without communication with the outside world.

I nodded. "Thank you."

2

To distract me, Anna and Britta wanted to train in the morning. I went along with their plan, but truth be told, I was too anxious and kept messing up. Taking pity on me, the sisters sent me for a shower and later let me help them with lunch—a miracle, as they always claimed the kitchen for themselves.

I made the salad, set the table, and washed whatever I could, and finally, at twelve thirty-eight, Britta's phone pinged.

"They are here," she said.

I rushed to the front door, the sisters right behind me and Shade nearby.

A gray SUV approached on the long driveaway, pulling to a stop in front of the porch.

A middle-aged witch hopped down. "Hi there," she said with a smile.

Britta and Anna waved at her. "Sonya, hi," Anna said. "Everything okay during the trip?"

"Oh, yeah," Sonya said as she rounded the car. "Boring, even." She opened the back door, and I sucked in a sharp breath.

My mother and sister sat with their backs straight and eyes wide and unseeing. My chest constricted.

Sonya gently touched my mother's hand. "We're here."

She tugged and my mother came with her. Then, she helped Amanda out. Both of them looked around for a few seconds, until their gaze found me.

"Hazel, there you are," my mother said, her voice almost robotic. A lump lodged in my throat as I walked toward them. "What a strange house. It sure needs some love."

Amanda tilted her head. "Oh, there is a house."

I glanced at Sonya. "Is this part of the spell?"

Sonya nodded. "I didn't want to turn them into over-sized dummies. They are still themselves, but dulled."

"Can you undo it?"

"Of course." The witch snapped her fingers.

My mother and Amanda blinked. They stared at me.

"What's going on?" my mother demanded.

"Where are we?" Amanda narrowed her eyes at the house. Of course, she was seeing it as I saw it the first time I came here—an abandoned, haunted-looking mansion.

"Hazel? Aren't you supposed to be at the Light Castle?" My mother looked at Sony, Anna, Britta, and Shade. "Who are these people?"

"I'll explain everything," I said. "Come inside with me."

"Inside? The house is falling apart," Amanda complained.

"It won't. You'll see." I guided them toward the front door. Halfway, I turned to Sonya. "Thank you."

She nodded. "No worries."

My mother, Amanda, and I entered the house as the sisters talked to Sonya. Shade stayed outside, probably sensing I needed time alone with them.

In the foyer, my mother and sister halted, their eyes huge as they took the place in.

"Holy shit," Amanda muttered.

My mother slapped her hand. "Language!" Then, she reached for me. "What is this place, Hazel? Why are we here? And more importantly, why is it that I can't remember leaving my house and coming here?"

I sighed and gestured toward the living room. It was only when they had a seat on the couch and I took an armchair, that I started. "There's no easy way to tell you everything."

"You're scaring me," my mother said.

Amanda huffed. "What mess did you get yourself into?"

I took a deep breath, ignoring my sister's jab. "I'm the reincarnation of Arianna, the founder of the Lightgrove coven. The three people you saw outside? They are Anna and Britta, Arianna's best friends, and Shade, her familiar, who has been able to shapeshift for the last six hundred plus years. Sean is upstairs; he is actually Prince Thales's reincarnation."

They stared at me, their mouths agape, their eyes wide, unblinking.

So, I went on. "Even before I found out, things were

crazy. I was captured by the Brotherhood, almost kidnapped by dark witches, Sean turned evil, and we went to Europe to recover my necklace and my grimoire. You remember the legend, right? About the items?"

"Are you freaking kidding me right now?" Amanda snapped.

"Hazel, that's not funny," my mother said, her voice low.

"You don't believe me." Why would they? My magic had always been subpar, and suddenly I was a legend.

My mother shook her head. "All right, Hazel, that's enough; tell us what's going on."

If they wouldn't believe me, then I could try something else. I rose from the chair, went to them, pushed them apart, and squeezed between them. "Give me your hands."

My mother sighed but relented. Amanda raised her eyebrows at me. "What are you trying to pull?"

"Just do it," I said, irritated.

Amanda rested her hand in mine.

And it was immediate. We were transported to the past, to the same house I had seen us in before.

My mother baked one of her famous sweet breads, while Aurelia sewed an old dress that had a small rip in the waist.

I was at the table, writing in my grimoire, and Shade was at my feet, purring and demanding attention.

A knock came at the door.

"Aren't you going to answer?" Amanda asked.

"I'm busy," I said, my focus on the spell I was creating. I did that a lot back then.

Grumbling, she put everything down, went to the door, and

opened it. "I should have known." She returned to her seat as Anna, Britta, and Jewell walked in.

Anna strode right in. "Good afternoon."

"Hi, girls," my mother said. She picked up a loaf of bread and a knife. "Here, have some bread."

Britta went directly to her. "Don't mind if I do."

Jewell crouched down beside me to pester Shade. He never liked her and that was why Jewell provoked him.

Anna leaned over my shoulder. "Another spell? What does this one do?"

"It should—"

"Does it matter?" Aurelia cut me off. "Whatever she does, she succeeds."

I glared at her before turning to my friends. "I thought we were meeting later tonight."

"We were but we intercepted a message for you." With a half-eaten slice of bread in one hand, Britta showed me the letter in the other. "The king summoned you."

Amanda pulled her hand from mine and the memory faded from behind my eyes. I blinked and found her pouting beside me.

My mother, though, watched with huge eyes filled with tears. "By the light." She held both my hands. "You are Arianna." She pulled me into a hug. "My dear daughter. How's that possible?"

"Anna and Britta couldn't bring me back, so they performed a spell for me to be reincarnated," I told her. "Though I don't think they expected it to take seven hundred years."

She pulled back and cupped my face. A tear rolled down her cheek. "That's amazing."

"It is, but that's just the beginning." I sighed and she dropped her hands. "The Brotherhood and the dark witches want me."

My mother went still. "Why?"

"I don't know all the details yet, but yes, I think we're going to have a fight on our hands."

"But ..." Her eyes filled with tears again. "You can't. You're ..."

"I'm Arianna and I'm regaining my powers." I could see how this subject was distressing her, so I decided to stop for now. Later, I would talk to her about the rest. "How about we continue this conversation later? Anna and Britta made lunch for us and it's probably getting cold."

I stood, but my mother remained seated for a minute. I looked pleadingly at Amanda. She stood, stared at me as if I was a stranger, and marched to the backyard.

That went well.

EVENING THAT DAY, I WALKED AROUND THE FRENCH Quarter, weaving through the crowd of people and tourists coming, going, and dancing, and talking, and eating. It was Tuesday after Thanksgiving, and this place was lively as ever.

I had a black hoodie covering my hair and kept my head low, but it wasn't necessary. Before we left the house, I had cast a spell to make our features different to whoever looked at us. Unless a supernatural of immense power focused directly on us, no one would recognize us.

Still, Anna and Britta had magically dyed their hair, Sean wore a hoodie, and Shade donned sunglasses and a baseball hat. The four of them walked several feet behind me, spread out through the street, watching for threats.

I hadn't invited Sean but he had asked to come.

"It'll keep my mind busy," he had said in a faint voice, his eyes not meeting mine.

This should be easy and quick, but in case something went sideways, it was always good to know he had my back.

As we walked, I couldn't help thinking of my mother and Amanda. During lunch, they acted strange, and my mother was polite to Anna and Britta. Sean had come down to get his plate, and after a half-assed hi to my family, he retreated to his suite. I talked to them again after lunch, while the sisters cleaned the kitchen. I made them promise me that until everything was said and done, they wouldn't leave the house. If they needed anything, they could ask us, and we would get it. Amanda grumbled and my mother cried, but both of them agreed.

Pushing those thoughts away for now, I stopped in front of the small bookstore at Dauphine Street. It was a narrow, three-story building with a small window displaying a selection of thick, old books. Cobwebs and dust spread over the books, and I wondered if that was decoration, even though Halloween was way past gone, or if this place was abandoned.

After a quick glance over my shoulder to check on my people, I went in.

A musky, moldy scent hit my nose and I almost gagged. This smell didn't go well with books. The door closed by itself behind me, and I glanced around. The bookstore was the width of the entire building, narrow and long, with bookshelves from floor to ceiling covering the walls, and a few hanging lights in between.

I picked up my phone and glanced at the text. Following the instructions, I walked to the middle of the building where there was a narrow set of stairs. I went up one floor and headed to the end of the building where there were three doors. I was told to go in the last one, which had a bronze plaque saying, "private studying room."

I opened the door and relaxed a little bit. Sadie was right there, inside the oddly bright room, seated at the desk, her eyes on the book in her hands.

She looked up and smiled at me. "There you are." She got up as I stepped into the room and closed the door behind me. "It's so nice to see you."

"You too." I lowered my hoodie and glanced at the only window in the room; it faced the back wall of another building. "What is this place?"

"Oh, it's a bookstore, but the owner is a widowed Light Order member who retired," Sadie said. "He still has connections inside the Lightgrove coven and sometimes lets the witches have meetings here."

"Does that mean you told someone about this meeting?" I had mentioned she couldn't tell anyone.

"Not exactly." She looked worried. "Only Fynn, and then Rodd when he followed us. They said they wouldn't ask questions as long as I allowed them to shadow me to make sure I'm okay." She tapped her fingers on the now closed book in front of her. It was a fantasy romance novel. "For a moment there, I was concerned this was some kind of trap."

I frowned. "Why would I trap you?"

She gestured to the chair across from the desk. "I don't know. The world is so crazy right now."

I sat down, apprehension making its way into my veins again. "Tell me what's going on? How's the situation in the Light Castle?"

Sadie leaned back in the chair, her expression closing. "After you ran away, things fell quickly." She lifted a finger. "I'm sure you're innocent, by the way, though some witches don't think you are."

"What are they saying about me?"

"That you helped the dark witch escape, and then you brought the entire Darkmist coven to attack us."

My breath stilled. "What?"

"Yeah, Queen Catarina and her witches attacked the Light Castle in the middle of the night. We fought with everything we had, but it was not enough. We fled."

"No," I whispered, stunned.

"We lost many witches and Light Order warriors. Queen Denise was gravely wounded, and despite all of our magic, we're not sure she's going to make it."

This couldn't be happening. "So, you're all in hiding?"

Sadie nodded. "We tried staying together, but it was too

dangerous. We've gathered in small groups and hid in and out of the city. We keep contact, though, just in case."

"And what's the plan? To retake the castle?"

"There's no plan. Our numbers are too small right now, lots of witches are afraid, and our queen is dying. Only Lenora and Clara are still alive. Well, Grace is missing. We don't know what happened to her. But Lenora and Clara don't want to ask for help from other covens." She tsked. "We're wasting time. The longer we wait, the more doubt and fear will snake into our hearts. Soon, we'll be useless."

"But you can't rush into the Light Castle head on," I said, and Sadie nodded. "Queen Catarina must be expecting that and she's probably ready. Besides, now she's closer to the coven's heart. She'll be stronger." And the Lightgrove will be weaker.

My brows knotted. Would Queen Catarina know where the heart was hidden? She was probably looking for it right now. And there were my ashes. They were also hidden in the castle. What if she found them accidentally? I couldn't even consider that.

"We need to find a way to attack them and to win," Sadie said.

"I agree." But how?

She tilted her head. "Hazel, why did you run?"

I let out a long sigh. "It was Grace. She tricked me."

I told her about Grace being a witch from the Ashmist coven, not the Lightgrove or the Darkmist, and how she wanted to unite her witches back to form the Lightmist coven once again. How apparently, despite kidnapping me and framing me, she wasn't bad and wanted to belong. I also told Sadie how Grace died during a battle with Queen Catarina, who had come to take me.

"Wait." Sadie narrowed her eyes. "You've met the Darkmist Witch Queen? And she wanted you? Why?"

I hesitated. The moment I made up my mind to call Sadie, I knew I would have to reveal the truth to her.

"You know how we hear stories that if someone recovers Queen Arianna's necklace, grimoire, and ashes, they can resurrect her?"

"Yes."

"Well, that isn't entirely true. When Anna and Britta realized they couldn't resurrect Arianna, they cast a powerful spell so she would be reincarnated instead, and her items would help her regain her memories and her power."

"Oh-kay." Sadie frowned. "I don't understand."

"Sadie ... Britta and Anna are still alive, Arianna's familiar is too, and he can shapeshift into a human, and Arianna was reincarnated eighteen years ago." Almost nineteen now.

I saw her face transformed from confusion to understanding in a matter of three seconds. "Oh my goodness." She pressed a hand to her mouth. "You're ... you're Arianna?"

It was half a question, half a statement.

I nodded. "Yes, I'm Arianna. And I've got my necklace and my grimoire back, and about sixty-ish percent of my memories and my power back." She stared at me, her eyes the size of oranges. "Oh, and Thales was also reincarnated ... as Sean."

"No way!" She let out a strangled laugh and then forced herself to be all serious again. "By the light, I should address you as your majesty or—"

"Don't be stupid," I said quickly. "I might be Arianna, but I still feel more like Hazel. Besides, our coven has a queen."

"But she's dying."

"Maybe I can help her. Or Britta and Anna. They are *powerful*."

"Holy shit, I'll meet Britta and Anna. This is insane."

"It really is, but it'll also be what we need. With me, Anna, Britta, Shade, Sean, and what's left of the Lightgrove, we might stand a chance against the Darkmist." I frowned. "The Ashmist will help, and I'm not too proud to ask for help." I still owed the Wildthorn coven, but I bet Khalisa knew of other witches who would help us. "Oh, is Guinevere hiding with you?"

Sadie shook her head. "No, she went missing during the battle. She might have fallen, but we aren't sure. Why?"

"She is from the Ashmist." I bit the inside of my lips. "I bet she is hiding with her coven." I could try to contact her somehow. "And—"

The door burst open, and a startled Moira stood in the doorway.

"You!" She pointed her finger at me. I shot up, startled.

Fynn and Rodd rushed in a moment later. "Sorry, she was too fast," Fynn said. Then, he saw me. "Hazel?"

Rodd grabbed his mother's arm and pulled her back before she could jump at me. "You came to meet Hazel?" he asked Sadie.

"Yes." She looked at me. "Sorry, Hazel. I promise I didn't tell Moira—"

"You didn't have to tell me," Moira snapped. She jerked from Rodd's grip, but stood beside him, no sign that she would go for my throat at the moment. "I saw when you received the text. I didn't know who it was from, but I noticed you were acting suspicious. So, I followed when you three sneaked out." She looked at me. "And you're here. This should be good." She narrowed her eyes. "Go on. If you don't want me to arrest you right now, you're going to tell me what this is about."

Shit, this wasn't how I planned things to go, but maybe it was for the best.

I opened my mouth to say something, but footsteps echoed outside the room. A moment later, Anna, Britta, Sean, and Shade stood behind Fynn, Rodd, and Moira.

"What's going on?" Anna asked.

"It's okay, Anna. I'm fine," I told her. "They won't hurt me."

Sadie's eyes bugged. "This is Anna?" Then she looked at her sister. "And you're Britta?"

"Hi, there." Britta waved.

"What?" Moira looked at the sisters. "What are you talking about?"

Oh, here we go again.

"Moira." I took two steps forward and touched her crossed arms. My intention was to undo the knot and force her to relax, but the moment I touched her, I was transported somewhere else.

A fist pounded on the door of the small house I lived in with my mother and sister, and I rushed to open it. This late at night, the pounding could only mean unwelcome news.

I unlocked the door and flung it open. On the other side stood a woman who looked exactly like Moira, but here in the past, she was Marion. She had hated me from the moment she first laid eyes on me. She had defied me when I wanted to separate the covens. She had tested my patience and anger. But she was righteous, loyal, and capable.

Beside her was her son, Ron. He was one of the first young men Prince Thales had recruited for the Light Order, and the two got along well. I suspected that trust and loyalty would be tested if Ron found out about Thales and I. Ron had made several public advances on me, and I had refused him, gently but firmly. If he knew Thales and I loved each other, I wondered how hurt he would be.

"What is it?" I asked, worried.

"She's here," Marion said, her eyes wide. "Jewell is coming with her witches."

I stilled. "Call an urgent meeting. We need to prepare."

Marion touched my arm and nodded.

I turned to Ron. "Send for the prince."

"Yes, my queen." Ron bowed and both of them dashed out into the night.

A sense of dread filled me.

I blinked and found myself back in the small studying room. I took a step back and stared at Moira, whose eyes swallowed her entire face.

"You ..." she started.

"You saw that?" I asked.

She nodded. "I ... give me a minute. I need to digest

this." She glanced around, her gaze landing again on Anna, Britta, Shade, and Sean. "Holy light, I can't believe it." She faced me again. "If you think because you're Queen Arianna that I'll apologize—"

I almost chuckled. "If you apologized, then I would think something is wrong with you." A small smile graced my lips. "You're the same." In appearance and personality. "You too," I said to Rodd.

He frowned. "What are you two talking about? Queen Arianna?"

"Hazel is Queen Arianna," Sadie said, sounding proud. "Sean is Prince Thales, and those are Anna, Britta, and Arianna's familiar, Shade." The sisters waved at them, Shade still wore the sunglasses inside, and Sean stood back, several feet away from everyone, looking as if he wanted to run from this place.

Fynn's eyes bugged. "What the hell? Is that true?"

I nodded. "It is. But most importantly is that we'll help you fight the Darkmist. We'll reclaim the Light Castle and restore order." Fynn frowned. Rodd stood at attention, as if ready for battle. I looked at Moira. "Can I count on you?"

Her eyes fixed on mine, and for a moment, I thought she wouldn't answer. "Always."

3

———

MOIRA, SADIE, FYNN, AND RODD LEFT AFTER PROMISING they would be ready and would do whatever I told them to. A small but heavy flower bloomed in my chest—responsibility. I was suddenly at the head of this whole thing, and I was supposed to lead our witches into battle. I felt insecure, inadequate, and weak.

As we walked out of the bookstore, I pulled my hoodie up and inhaled deeply. Arianna had been strong, fearless, and determined. She hadn't been perfect by any means, but she had done her best until the end. I didn't feel one hundred percent like her yet, but I would draw as much as I could from those memories and believe that I would make this work somehow.

Outside, Sean barely stopped to hear me. He walked into the crowd and disappeared. My heart sank.

Shade followed my line of sight. "I'll keep an eye on him." And he followed Sean.

"Are you okay?" Anna asked.

"Last time Sean and Shade were alone, they were kidnapped by Grace and her witches."

"Don't worry," Britta said. "I bet they are on high alert right now and won't do anything stupid."

"They're probably walking toward the car right now." Anna hooked her arm through mine. "We'll meet them there."

"Actually, I want to stop by Khalisa if that's okay," I said. I wanted to see how she was doing, what she knew about what was going on, and also to send a message to Queen Yira that I hadn't forgotten about her wand, and I would help her soon.

Anna and Britta exchanged that unnerving glance of theirs. I knew they didn't do it on purpose, and I knew that for being sisters and living together for over seven hundred years, their bond was incredible, so I tried cutting them some slack about it.

Britta nodded. "We should be quick."

She walked a few steps in front of us, her head snapping to one side and the other, looking for any threats.

Khalisa's shop was two short blocks away and we got there without any trouble.

The sisters and I entered the shop, and the heavy scent of herbs and incense filled the air.

Khalisa turned to us with a smile on her lips. "Welcome to—" Her dark eyes widened and her face paled. "Child, you shouldn't be here."

I frowned. "Hi to you too."

"No, I'm serious. It isn't safe." She hurried to me and pushed me toward the door. "Leave now."

Anna and Britta crowded behind me. "What's going on? What are you afraid of?" Anna asked.

Khalisa shook her head, the white beads at the end of her long dreadlocks jiggling with the movement. "They know you come here often, and they are watching."

"Who?" Britta asked.

The door opened behind us, and five witches walked in. The sisters, Khalisa, and I scooted back, putting distance between us—an almost impossible task inside the cluttered shop.

Instantly, I recognized the one in the front. She had been with Queen Catarina the night she turned Sean into a demon.

"Dear Hazel, or should I call you Queen Arianna?" she said and I froze. It was still unsettling when someone referred to me like that. "Finally, we meet properly. Let me introduce myself. I'm Princess Gillian, second in command of the Darkmist coven."

"What do you want?" Anna snapped.

"I'm here for Hazel, of course," Gillian said with a smile. Her eyes never left mine. "My queen demands your presence. You can come peacefully, or ... not." She glanced at her long black nails as if bored. "And just so you know before you start making plans, I have a dozen more witches surrounding this place. You have nowhere to go."

"I'm afraid I can't go," I said with as much sarcasm as I could manage. "Tell your queen I have another appointment."

Gillian's smile stretched even more. "What are you afraid of, Hazel? That Queen Catarina will kill you? I can assure you that's not the case. At least, not right away." She chuckled. "No, she wants to talk to you. You see, she has a story to share with you."

What could Queen Catarina want to tell me? "I'm sure nothing she has to say interests me." Behind me, I could feel Anna and Britta calling their powers, getting ready to attack.

"Oh, but she has." One of the other witches said, her voice as malicious as Gillian's.

Gillian cut her a glare. "Shush."

The young witch recoiled, as if she was preparing for a slap.

"That's Robin," Khalisa whispered to me. "Queen Catarina's daughter. She's about your age."

Gillian returned her gaze to me, the young witch forgotten. "I can give you a preview," she continued. "Queen Catarina is a direct descendant of one of Arianna's best friends and she has her grimoire and her diary, which contains all sorts of goodie details about the past. I've read it and it's ... insightful."

"What are you—?"

The world spun and I found myself in the palace's library with Anna, Britta, and Jewell. We were all hunched over a long table, writing in our grimoires. Except for Jewell ... she had switched her grimoire for her diary.

"What happened that is so interesting?" Anna asked. She always teased Jewel for keeping a diary.

"So many things," Jewell answered without stopping. She

continued writing furiously in her diary. "For example, right now I'm writing what a pain in the ass you are."

Britta laughed. "That she is."

Anna glared at her sister. "You're worse!"

Jewell chuckled. "You two take first place."

"What about me?" I asked.

She finally looked up from her diary. "You ... you might be in fourth, maybe fifth place."

I gasped. "And who took the second and third place from me?"

"My sister and Shade." She pointed her quill to the chair across from the table where Shade was curled up, sleeping.

I smiled. "He's a pain in the ass, but he is my pain in the ass."

Footsteps sounded outside the library, and we knew the prince and his guards were coming.

Jewel leaned closer to me. "And the prince is in first place for you?" She winked at me, and I elbowed her as Thales entered the library, his eyes landing on me.

My cheeks heated up.

The world revolved once again. Gillian looked at me with a puzzled expression. "What was that?"

"Nothing," I barked. I certainly wouldn't explain myself to her.

"You—"

A glass vial flew through the air in an arc and landed at Gillian's feet. Thick smoke quickly rose to the air.

"Run!" Khalisa yelled.

Anna and Britta grabbed my arms, pulling me to the back of the shop, while Khalisa stood in the way.

"What are you doing?" I asked her.

"Buying you time, child," she said.

"What? No!"

She looked at me, the most serious I had ever seen her. "You're too important. Go. Now. Please."

She pushed me back then turned toward the smoke.

"Wait," I called, but Anna and Britta had their hands around my arms and dragged me across the room, to the door that led to the back alley.

My limbs grew heavy and my mind spun. If Khalisa died ... I shook my head. No, I wouldn't think about that. She was strong and brave. Somehow, she would make it out of there.

We stopped before the back and Anna opened it. She spied out from a small crack, then she put her head out, and finally she stepped out. "It's clear. Let's go!"

We ran out of the shop into the narrow alley. Despite being the middle of the day, the buildings were too close together and tall, blocking most of the sunlight.

We didn't take ten steps toward one of the alley's entrances when witches ran in from both sides and surrounded us. Gillian wasn't joking when she said there were a dozen of them outside.

"Shit," Anna cursed.

"We can fight them," Britta said. "The three of us are probably stronger than all of them."

Anna nodded. "True."

There was no time for chitchat. The witches went straight for us, magic bolts flying left and right.

Anna threw light bolts like a mad woman, while Britta

raised a wall in front of us, keeping half of the witches busy as they tried breaking it.

"It won't hold for long!" she yelled as she turned to the other half and joined Anna in the fight.

For a moment, I stood frozen. The last fight I remembered I had killed a witch. I didn't want to kill anyone again, even if they were the evilest being in the entire world. There had to be ways of stopping them without killing them.

"Hazel, wake up!" Britta yelled as the wall broke, and the rest of the witches swarmed us.

I raised another shield, but it had been too fast, without thinking, and almost no power behind it. It took the witches another five seconds to break it.

I called my magic, knowing I would have to fight. I would hurt them, I would numb them, but I wouldn't kill them.

Four witches reached me, and I lifted my hands, ready to strike. The lightning crackled in my hands, and I threw a bolt at the closest one. The lightning hit her chest and she fell back, convulsing.

I stared at her, frozen.

Had I killed her?

A hand grabbed my arm and I yelped—then a black cat jumped on the back of the witch, making her let go of me. Shade shifted into his human form and took the witch's attention away from me. I took a step back, as if that was enough to avoid the other two ... one of them lifted her hand and threw a spark of magic at me.

I stood there.

Someone stepped in front of me with a long stick—Sean and ... was that a broomstick? He swung the stick like a bo staff and deflected the magic spark. I gawked at how fluidly he moved, how fast, how he avoided their magic, as if he had fought witches before.

It was Thales' memories.

Sean knocked them both out by hitting the stick hard on their heads. Fainted, not dead. He turned to me, his eyes scanning every inch of me.

"Are you okay?" There was an urgency in his voice, a desperation I hadn't heard in a while.

I nodded. He cupped my face and I almost cried. He hadn't touched me in days. "I know this is hard for you. It's hard for me too. But you need to fight, my love. We need to get out of this place now."

My eyes on his, I grabbed his wrist, inhaled deeply, and nodded.

For him, for us, for what Arianna and Thales had been, I pushed away my fear and my worries. I focused on the powerful magic inside of me, in the necklace resting at my collarbone.

I channeled my power and sent a huge wave of lighting across the alley. It hit everyone—except for Anna, Britta, Shade, Sean, and me—and sent them flying back a handful of feet. Some witches fell unconscious, others were too hurt to move for a few seconds.

And that was enough for us to run.

"Let's go!" Anna shouted.

We sped to the alley's mouth. Shade transformed into a cat and sprinted ahead of us. We joined in the French

Quarter craziness, but no one paid attention to us. A minute later, Shade appeared with the car on a side street. Without a word, we got into the car and Shade drove away.

I looked back and despite not seeing anything, I could feel eyes on us.

4

Shade didn't drive straight to the house, afraid that we were being followed. Instead, he drove around New Orleans for one hour and we stopped once so the sisters could change the car's color and plate with magic.

Worried, I called Khalisa.

"I'm glad you're okay, child," she said. And I was glad she was okay too. She told me the dark witches broke a few things in her shop, but since their interest was on me, they left her alone pretty quick. She promised she wasn't hurt.

"What can we do about your shop?" I asked, feeling guilty.

"Don't worry, child. This is all material, most of it is fake and easily replaceable. I'll take the day to clean up today, and the store should be open again tomorrow."

I apologized again, but she shushed me.

First, I broke Queen Yira's wand, now I destroyed Khalisa's shop. What else would I ruin in this quest?

At the house, we gathered in the kitchen where the

sisters examined us for wounds and scratches. My mother went ballistic when we told her about the attack and she prepared us some quick healing tea—infused with Anna's magic, since my mother's was weak.

After grabbing his mug, Sean went upstairs. He hadn't touched me, spoke to me, or even glanced my way since that tender moment in the alley.

I hated this.

But there was a more pressing issue I needed to solve first.

After my mother doted on me and made sure I was okay, I leaned on the kitchen's counter and faced the sisters. Anna was gathering ingredients to make more tea, and Britta and my mother were already discussing dinner. Shade had gone outside with a second mug of tea, and Amanda was probably in her bedroom. She had barely left it after I told them the truth about my past.

"We need to talk," I said. The sisters stilled and then exchanged that damned glance.

My mother cleared her throat. "I'll ... I'll leave you to it." She took a good look at me, then walked upstairs, probably to check on my sister.

Once she was gone, I continued. "No excuses, no arguments. Just ... talk to me, answer my questions. I have most of my memories back. I need you to fill in the blanks with the truth. For our friendship, for everything you've done for me for the last seven hundred years, can you do that? Can you tell me the truth?"

Again, that glance. It irritated me to no end.

Anna and Britta nodded. They leaned on the kitchen

island, a couple of feet from me, and faced me.

"What do you want to know?" Britta asked.

"So many things," I said. "I want to know the real reason why I split the Lightmist, and why it doesn't seem like I was as pure and innocent as everyone seems to think."

Anna let out a long breath. "It was because of Jewell. You've seen her in your visions. Like you, she was one of the rare witches who were born to light witches but had a dark gift. She was two years younger than you, and she absolutely idolized you."

"At first, she was an annoying kid who followed us around, who pestered you, but you were always good-hearted." Britta smiled. "Slowly, you took her in, and our little group went from three to four. She was our little mascot. We took care of her and taught her all we knew."

"Her parents were mean to her, because of her dark magic, so we became her family," Anna said, her tone somber. "When dark witches started getting together and creating subgroups to attack the Brotherhood of Purity, Jewell started changing. She was interested in what was happening, and she wanted news of the witches and the Brotherhood and the witch hunts. She sent messages to other towns and villages. She even contacted the Lightmist witch queen, asking for an audience to discuss the future of the dark witches. The queen replied saying the dark witches would be punished for causing so much trouble and bringing the Brotherhood to their doorstep."

"The three of us started arguing with her when she seemed too focused on the dark witches," Britta said.

"Then, one day, she disappeared. We searched for her, asked around, sent word to other covens and witches, but no one had seen or heard from her. Right at that time, the war between the dark witches and the Brotherhood intensified. The witch hunts spread. Even light witches were being found and killed."

"Innocent, magicless human women were being hunted and killed," Anna added. "You needed to look at someone the wrong way, and you're a suspect of witchcraft. Any small excuse was a good reason to either burn a woman at the stake or hang her."

"A few months later, Jewell came back," Britta said. "She was changed. She looked different. She let her dark hair grow to her knees, she dressed in all black, wore dark makeup, and she was rude to us from the moment she walked in the door and back into our lives."

Anna, Britta, and I were preparing to leave for the castle as we had a meeting with the king about my next mission. And then Jewell burst in the door like a dark tornado.

"Jewell!" I said, happy to see her again. But that feeling only lasted three seconds. The moment I took her in—her hard expression, her posture, the wildness in her dark eyes—I knew this wasn't the same Jewell who had been one of my best friends. "What happened?"

"I couldn't stay in your shadows," she said. "I couldn't stand hearing about witches who are like us being hunted and killed by the Brotherhood. I had to do something. I joined them. I made them stronger, more organized, and we faced the Brotherhood. Right now, my witches are running around this village, gathering all dark witches who want to join us." She grabbed

my hands in hers. "Join us. You all should join us. If the light witches stand with us, the Brotherhood won't win. We'll kill every single one of them, and all of their sympathizers." She squeezed my hands. "Hell, those bullies from when we were little? We can take them all down too. We'll kill everyone who ever wronged us. We'll be the strongest coven to ever walk this Earth."

I pulled my hands from hers and took two big steps back. "Jewell, I don't think you hear yourself. You're talking about killing innocents, people who don't deserve it."

"They don't deserve it?" Her voice rose. "They humiliated us! They even beat some of us up! They deserve a slow and painful death. We'll rise up, be known everywhere, and even humans will know us. They will fear and bow to us."

I shook my head as despair filled my veins. I was losing my friend. "The queen will never approve of this. You'll be expelled from the coven."

One corner of her lips curled up. "The queen won't have a say."

I inhaled sharply. "Jewell ... what did you do?"

"I prepared a trap," she said, sounding so proud. "I sent the queen and her heirs directly into the Brotherhood's arms. By now, she should be dead. Our coven needs a new queen."

I gasped. "No, you wouldn't have done that."

A loud knock came from the door. Jewell opened it. "Hi, Marion."

Marion frowned. "Jewell, you're back?" She shook her head. "That's not important." Jewell's nostrils flared and her eyes darkened. Marion went on, "Arianna, a note arrived for you. It was half open, so I read it." She handed me the note.

I read it and my heart sank. "The queen and her daughters are dead. We lost our queen." I looked at Jewell, my heart breaking. "How could you do this?"

I blinked and stared at Anna's and Britta's worried faces.

"Are you back?" Anna asked and I nodded. "We realized you were having a memory. What did you see?"

"The continuation of what you were telling me," I said, my voice low. My heart hurt as if it had been yesterday. Jewell, one of my best friends, had become evil. She was killing innocents and she had killed our witch queen. "When Jewell came back, and Marion told us the queen was dead."

Britta nodded. "I remember that day."

"And I remember now what happened after."

As much as I tried, Jewell didn't back down. She was intent on taking over the coven with or without me, and attack everyone and everything who stood in her way. Quickly, her vision expanded. She now wanted to become queen of Europe, cull the humans, and have the ones who were left as slaves.

And she started by attacking our village.

I didn't let her. I gathered the lights witches from the village and Prince Thales' army, and we battled against her. It was a quick, but bloody thing, and in the end, Jewell and her witches retreated with the promise to come back another day. She also promised to send the Brotherhood after me.

Jewell left behind pure chaos. Without much choice, I did what I felt like I should: I called on all light witches from our village and the surrounding towns and proposed we formed our own coven. With Anna's and Britta's help, I stormed the previous queen's mansion and stole the coven's heart before Jewell could. I hadn't really thought about it, but then I realized I was the new queen of a new coven made entire of light witches—except for me.

Our main motto was to be good, always, no matter what. To ourselves, to each other, to strangers, to the world. To help those in need, whoever they were. To be an example and do our best in any situation.

But as promised, Jewell sent the Brotherhood a few weeks later … and I was killed.

I shook my head, letting it all sink in.

"I was so naive and hypocritical," I finally whispered. "I was a dark witch, and I pushed the others away."

"You weren't like the others," Anna said quickly. "We knew not all dark witches were like Jewell, but the large majority was, and the ones who weren't, were too afraid and hid from her and from us."

"And from the Brotherhood," Britta reminded us. "Their efforts were focused on dark witches since they were the ones wreaking havoc, but they never stopped hunting us too."

Us. As if I was a light witch like all of them.

But I had never been. And I wasn't one now.

Yet, I had made myself queen of the light witches.

By the light, I had been so stupid!

"Hazel." Anna walked toward me but stopped two feet away. "What you did was good. You saved so many innocent witches fr—"

"And human women too," Britta added.

"Right." Anna nodded. "Innocent witches and human women from being killed. Thousands, for sure. You had the courage to do what no one else even thought of, and it was our salvation. Don't overthink this for one second."

"Anna is right. You did what you had to, and we were so proud of being your friends, and helping you. We are so proud still." Britta walked closer too, and rested her hand on my arm. "I'm sorry we didn't tell you all of this before. We were afraid that realizing this side of you too early would impact what you need to do now."

I inhaled deeply. "And what do I need to do now?" I knew the answer, but hearing someone else saying it, realizing I wasn't the only crazy one in the bunch, would help.

"You need to get your ass in gear and defeat the Darkmist witches," Anna said. "You need to reclaim the Light Castle, and if they come for us, you need to show the Brotherhood they shouldn't mess with us."

I huffed. "The Brotherhood is everywhere in the world. We can't defeat them all."

"No, but if we can scare the New Orleans group into silence, won't that be worth it?" Britta asked with a new mischievous glint in her eyes.

That was a lot. Truth be told, once they told me who I was and I started remembering, I knew this day would come. Otherwise, why would I even have resurrected? Just to live longer? That was so selfish.

No, I was here for a higher purpose. I had helped innocent witches before. I would do it again.

I rolled my shoulders and puffed out my chest. "If we do this, we'll need help."

I WROTE ON THE BACK OF THE NOTE GRACE LEFT FOR ME. The words disappeared after a minute. Another minute passed and new words appeared on the paper: *Let's meet tomorrow afternoon.*

I would have rather talked on the phone, but I knew those were easily hacked nowadays, and even though our world was sometimes slow to catch up with technology, I didn't doubt witches, or even the Brotherhood, had a hacker in their midst.

I couldn't sleep; the past, the future, the problems in the present plagued me. The Darkmist, the Ashmist, the Lightgrove coven. The fact that Queen Denise was critically injured and probably wouldn't make it.

And the one fact that hurt the most: knowing Sean was a few doors down and I couldn't even go to him.

Tired of tossing and turning, I hopped out of the bed and tiptoed to the kitchen downstairs. I turned on the dim lights under the counter and started gathering ingredients to make a sleeping tea with maybe some infused magic, when I saw a faint light coming from the window outside.

My heart skipped a beat, and I froze.

Was it dark witches? The Brotherhood?

Then the back door opened, and Sean stepped inside the kitchen, his phone in his hand, the screen on. He saw me and halted, the door half closed.

"I'm sorry," he said, closing the door. He dashed across the kitchen.

"For what?" I asked.

He stopped and looked at me. "What?"

"What are you sorry for?"

He glanced around, then let out a long breath, and faced me. "I don't know. For disrupting whatever you're doing. For being in the way. For—"

"Sean," I said with a sigh. "Just ... you're not disrupting anything. Only my soul and my pride because you act as if I disgust you."

His eyes widened. "I've already told you." He took a step closer then stopped again. "Hazel, you should be the one disgusted with me. You should be scared of me. You should be mad at me. You should hate me for all I've done, for the way I treated you."

"It wasn't you."

"But it was. Queen Catarina said that her spell awakened the fun parts in me and pushed the rest away. Everything you saw was always there, but they weren't this pronounced, this strong, this dominating. It was like the evil side of me was the only side." His brows knotted, and he looked pained. "I can't erase that, Hazel. I'm not a hundred percent evil, but I still feel it. Now that it is awake, that it was used, my dark side is pulsing, waiting, pushing for me to use it again." His voice lowered. "I'm not sure how long I can ignore it."

I set the herbs down and went to him. I could see he wanted to run, he wanted to step back, but I was glad he stood his ground. However, I didn't want to push him. I knew the others were right. He needed time, and I intended to give it to him.

"The experience you went through ..." I shook my head. "I can't imagine. And now feeling that dark seed inside of you and having to fight it all the time, it can't be easy. But Sean ... I'm here for you. Now and forever. You can lean on me. Allow me to help you, to share this burden with you, and—"

"I can't do that to you." He shook his head. "I won't taint you with my darkness."

I almost chuckled. "I'm a light witch with dark magic, Sean. I'm already touched by darkness." He frowned. Prince Thales had known about Arianna's powers, but I wasn't sure if Sean had remembered yet and I honestly didn't remember telling him. "I'm not comparing your experience to mine, but I want you to see that together, we'll be stronger."

He stared at me, his blue eyes shining in the dim light. Damn, he was so handsome. His sharp jaw ticked as he clenched his teeth. "I ..." He shook his head once, took a large step back. "Good night, Hazel."

Without another word or another glance, Sean hurried upstairs to his room, and I was left alone in the kitchen.

Tears burned behind my eyes.

Rejection hurt, especially when I knew we belonged together. But I wouldn't be a pushy girlfriend. I wouldn't do that to him. He needed space. All right, he would have it.

I turned back to my herbs and made the tea stronger— I would need it.

Not sleeping well was becoming the norm and I didn't like it. I was waking up grumpy and only an unholy amount of food appeased my mood. Thankfully, my mother and the sisters were great cooks and always had something delicious ready.

In the morning, my mother cleaned the house, though I had told her she didn't need to, and Anna, Britta, and I practiced in the backyard for a few hours. It was a safe way to spend the time, get the rust out of our bones, and come up with plans for retaking the Light Castle.

After our training, I went up to my bedroom for a shower before lunch, and as I walked past a window overlooking the front garden, I saw Sean running across the driveaway in his running clothes. It seemed he also wanted to burn off some energy.

I knew other ways we could pass the time and burn energy together. My stomach clenched at the thought of making love to him, and a deep ache hollowed in my chest at the prospect that he might never recover, and we wouldn't ever be together again.

As I expected, Sean didn't come back for lunch. I think he did it on purpose, so he wouldn't have to sit with us. Instead, he came in later, after my mother had cleaned the kitchen, served himself leftovers, heated it up in the microwave, and took it to his room to eat.

Sometimes, tiny things could ignite my blood and I wanted to scream at him: Why the hell did he bother to stay here if he wouldn't even acknowledge us?

But I knew the answer. It was as dangerous out there for him as it was for me. Even if he never talked to us again —to me—it would be better if he stayed here.

Thirty minutes before our meeting, Shade drove the sisters and me to the lake's edge in a state park outside New Orleans.

When he stopped in the parking lot, Shade said he would stay by the car in case we needed a quick exit again. All we had to do was throw a magic spark into the air and he would know we had to go fast.

The sisters exited the car and came with me into the park. It was the middle of the afternoon, and despite the chilly air—I was glad I had chosen a thicker jacket than my usual leather one—a few people were here. Some had a picnic blanket on the grass, some walked the trails and paths, others biked, and some parents watched their kids at the playground.

But almost no one stood by the lake's edge.

Only Guinevere.

I hadn't seen her in a couple of weeks. Her white porcelain skin seemed flushed in the sun, the orange in her hair was almost gone, and that easy smile that always made me think of her more like a friend than a mentor was nowhere to be seen.

She saw us coming and her posture straightened.

"She seems to have come alone," Anna said, her gaze darting from side to side. She stopped walking. "Britta and I will stay behind, but in sight."

Britta stopped. "Just yell and we'll come for you."

I nodded and kept going.

The closer I got to Guinevere, the more I saw she looked older and wearier than before, as if the weight of the past few weeks had been too much for her. In the castle, she wore an elegant suit or ballgown, but today she was dressed in slacks, a thin sweater, and a jacket. Her familiar, a small squirrel, was in the breast pocket of her jacket.

"Hello, Hazel," she said as I halted a handful of steps from her. "Hm, I hope you're well."

"As well as one can be with everything going on."

Her brows knotted. "Would you prefer if I called you Queen Arianna?"

I shook my head. I bet the entire Ashmist coven knew who I was. "No, please. I'm no queen." I wasn't one back then, though the crown had fallen on my head anyway. "Hazel is fine."

"Hazel sounds good."

I pursed my lips. "I'm sorry about Grace and Starla and the others who died that night."

"And I'm sorry Grace liked theatrics." Her voice was

low and serious. "If she hadn't gone around in circles and played with you so much, maybe she and the others would still be here. Maybe Catarina wouldn't have invaded the Light Castle and attacked the light witches." She sighed. "Unfortunately, even with our powers, we can't change the past. We can only prepare and make a better future."

I nodded. "That night, Grace told me her wish was for the light witches to realize that not all dark witches are evil. She wished the Lightgrove witches would welcome the Ashmist witches back and create a more powerful coven, one that would certainly be stronger than the Darkmist."

"That is the wish of all Ashmist witches," Guinevere said. "Right now, we live in limbo. We're not dark enough, but we are rejected by the light covens. We are hunted, though all we want is to exist in peace. Or at least, in peace inside our supernatural society—fighting the bad guys and doing good."

Doing good. That was the motto Arianna had envisioned for the Lightgrove coven.

"Speaking of fighting bad guys, I want to attack the Darkmist and drive them away from the Light Castle."

"And you want my coven's help."

I nodded. "I need your help. Without you and your witches, we won't have enough power to defeat them."

She stared at me for a moment. "We'll help you and fight the Darkmist witches ... on one condition: we join the Lightgrove coven for good."

I knew this was coming. "Queen Denise is still alive along with two other council members, and—"

"You're the real queen of the Lightgrove coven."

"I won't take the title away from the current queen." I didn't even think I wanted it. "But because of who I was, I'm sure they will make me a council member." And if they didn't, I would demand it. I bet most witches would agree with that. "I give my word that I will do everything in my power to reintegrate the Ashmist into the Lightgrove."

Guinevere extended her hand to me. "That's good enough for me."

6

THE SUN WAS SETTING WHEN WE MADE IT BACK TO THE enchanted house.

"Dinner will be ready in about an hour," my mother said from the kitchen as we walked in the house.

"What's for dinner?" Shade asked.

"Lasagna," my mother answered. "From scratch."

"Make that one and a half hours," Britta said. She and Anna headed to the kitchen, undoubtedly to help my mother. I didn't know how the three of them didn't argue with so many people calling the shots in there.

I offered to help them, mostly to be polite, and thankfully the three of them shooed me out of the kitchen.

"It's their thing," Shade said. He twirled the car keys with his finger. "Cooking. They learned it after you and Prince Thales were gone, when we moved to Venopolis. That was when they were keeping to themselves for a while, trying to come with a good plan, but they found themselves with a lot of time on their hands."

"Thus, the cooking."

He nodded. "Back then, it took a lot longer, but there wasn't such variety." His nose wrinkled. "In the beginning, they were terrible at it."

I smiled. "And you were their guinea pig."

He smiled too. "I was. Thankfully, they got better."

We heard footsteps on the stairs. A second later, Sean walked into the living room. His gaze met mine, then rummaged all over me. "You're back and well. I take it went all right?"

I frowned. "Yes."

"Good." He turned and marched away.

"Wait," I called, took a step toward him then stopped.

"What are you doing?" Shade asked me. "Go after him."

"But he needs space." I repeated the mantra that played nonstop inside my head.

"He came downstairs to make sure you're okay." Shade raised an eyebrow. "Now it's your turn. Go see if he's okay."

Smart cat. I smiled at him again and raced up the stairs after Sean.

When I got to the second floor, Sean was already in front of his bedroom door.

"Wait," I called. But of course, he didn't. He went in and started closing the door. I ran—Amanda's bedroom door was closed, as usual—and pushed on the door as it was about to close. "Seriously?" I asked, out of breath from my short sprint. "You can't stand being near me, so you need to run away this fast?"

Sean retreated several steps, stopping in the middle of

his room, right beside the bed. "We've been through this. It's not that."

I stood under the doorframe, afraid of scaring him away again. "Then what is that?"

He gritted his teeth. "I ... I needed to make sure you're okay. That's all."

I took one small step inside his room. "Why?"

"Hazel."

Another step. "I need to know. Why do you want to make sure I'm okay?"

"Don't do this."

Another step. "Why?"

He groaned, clenching his arms and making his muscles contract under his short-sleeve gray shirt. "You're not making it easy."

"If life was easy, it wouldn't be fun." I took one last step and halted right in front of him. I reached for him and laid my hand flat on his corded arm. "Sean ..."

The world spun and suddenly we were in the castle's library between two tall shelves full of books, standing directly in front of each other.

"You're not making it easy," Prince Thales said with a groan.

I knew exactly what this was about, but I feigned igno-rance. "What are you talking about?"

"You—" He clamped his mouth, pressing his lips into a thin line. His eyes searched mine, then dipped to my exposed neck, to my collarbone, and the not-so-modest cleavage of my dark green dress. He cursed under his breath, then his eyes met mine again.

"What about me?"

"You know very well what you do to me."

I leaned forward and looked up at him. "No, I don't."

He cursed again, his eyes glinting with pure desire. "That's it." He wrapped an arm around my waist, one hand around my nape, and he dipped his head to mine.

His lips crashed onto mine, and I gasped in delight.

I blinked and found Sean staring at me with that same glint in his eyes.

I swallowed. "Did you see that?"

Sean nodded. "That was the first time I kissed you. I had wanted to do that for so long, but until then, I was able to resist you."

"I'm glad you finally gave in."

"Me too." The words were so low, so faint, I almost believed he hadn't said anything.

"Sean." I slid my hand down his arm and knotted our fingers together. "Let me in. Give in again. Let me help you. I *want* to help you." I reached up and touched his cheek. "And I know that deep down, you want that too." He closed his eyes and leaned his face on my hand. "Give in to me."

Sean grabbed my arm, placed a kiss on my wrist, extracting a gasp from me, before wrapping his arms around me and pulling me to him. His mouth was on mine before I could make sense of anything, but right now I didn't want to.

All that mattered was that he was here with me, touching me, kissing me, loving me.

Breaking the kiss, Sean twisted us to his bed and gently deposited me on the mattress. He crawled over me and pressed his body against mine. I gasped as pure desire coursed through me.

Suddenly, he stilled, his brows furrowed. "I'm so sorry, Hazel. For all I've done when my dark side was in control."

I cupped his beautiful face. "You don't need to apologize, but if you feel like you have to, then know that I forgive you." I wound my legs around his hips and tugged him to me. "Now come here."

One corner of his lips curled up and then he dipped into me again and kissed me. At first, slow and deep, as if he needed to take his time to repent, but as I squirmed under him, rubbing my hips on his, sliding my hands under his shirt and scratching my nails on his skin, the kiss became more desperate. Faster, deeper, taking my breath away.

In another minute, our clothes were on the floor, and we were deliciously joined as one. Hopefully, this time nothing would break us apart again.

7

That evening, Sean joined us for dinner, and the sisters teased him for making me so miserable I was almost intolerable these past few days.

Dinner was a mix of casual, comfortable, and awkward as Sean wasn't fully himself yet. My guess was that the guilt and darkness would remain inside of him for a long time, and he would have to either learn how to live with it or learn how to ignore it.

After dinner, we all sat in the backyard around the fire pit and ate s'mores while talking about the past. Increasingly, Sean and I remembered our past lives, and everything made sense.

We also talked about the present. My mother and Amanda, who finally had gotten out of her bedroom and joined us, hadn't really met Sean until they moved in a couple of days ago, and they wanted to know all about him —his family, where he had grown up, his major in college —and he was glad to oblige them.

When it was bedtime, Sean stopped by his suite to brush his teeth and get his pajamas, but thankfully, he came to my bedroom. But we didn't sleep right away. No, we made love again, then snuggled in to sleep, and that was one of the best nights I had in a long time.

The next day, I felt refreshed, light, and ready to take on the world.

In the morning, Sean went out for a run while I trained with the sisters.

"I see things worked themselves out and you two are being all smoochie smoochie again," Anna teased as she threw a bolt of magic at me.

I swiped my hand, creating a small wave of lightning that bumped into her bolt and exploded on contact.

"By the light, tell me you won't be like your last life," Britta said. She sent five fast bolts at me, and I raised a barrier to take them on. "Once you two finally gave in, you couldn't take your hands off each other. It was annoying."

"It was, but it was also cute." Anna opened up her arms and a wave of magic came rolling toward me. "You two were made for each other."

Using the same motion Anna used, I parted the wave, sending it to the sides, but staying intact in the middle.

Britta nodded. "True. In the previous life and in this one."

My cheeks heated. Didn't I know that? Didn't I feel that? That was why I hadn't backed off from Sean. He had needed space, but I also knew he had needed me—my support, my help, my love. That was what would really heal him.

I channeled my lightning and created a storm within our circle. The sisters shielded themselves, but the lightning broke through in a few seconds and I had to control my magic not to hurt them for real.

Anna smiled at me, proud. "You're getting better and better."

"And that's not even your full power," Britta added.

I shuddered, not sure I wanted or deserved so much power. I was afraid that it would change me, that it would corrupt me. Deep down, though, I knew the power would be what I made of it, and all I had to do was lean on my friends and family.

I glanced at the house. My mother was at the kitchen door, drinking tea and watching us, a mix of panic and pride stamped on her face. Amanda was probably in her bedroom watching Netflix, like she had done for the past few days. She had been so upset when I told them who I was, who they were, she barely spoke to me. I sometimes wondered if I should push her, like I pushed Sean, and help her get past this wall that had been lifted between us.

After training, my mother helped the sisters with lunch. It was impossible for her to stay here and do nothing—I had even seen her gardening and cleaning the unused living room and office. Sean had already come back from his run, taken a shower, and was now waiting for me in the family room.

"I watched the last few minutes there and you're kicking ass," he said as I walked to him. He met me halfway and pressed a quick kiss on my lips.

I pulled back, knowing I was dirty, sweaty, and smelly,

and he was all clean and smelling wonderfully. "Let's hope it's enough."

He nodded. "It will be."

"Do you know if Amanda is still in her bedroom?"

"She was when I walked by about fifteen, twenty minutes ago."

"I'm going to go talk to her. Then I'm going to take a shower and—"

"Want some company?" He showed me that lopsided grin that made my stomach clench with anticipation.

"In the shower?" I asked and he nodded. "I thought you had taken a shower already."

"I don't think I would mind taking another one, especially if you're going to be there." He leaned into me, and this time, when he kissed me, I didn't pull away. His mouth closed over mine, and I melted into him, my body igniting. His hands snaked around my waist, and he pulled me to him.

I broke the kiss and stepped back, chuckling. "I'm all dirty."

He shrugged. "I thought I was going to take another shower soon."

"All right, Mr. Hot Tattooed Guy."

"What?" He seemed confused.

"That's what I called you in my head when we first met."

One of his eyebrows lifted, his eyes gleaming with mischief. "Really?"

"Really." I turned to the stairs before he kissed me again, and I skipped seeing my sister and went directly to the shower with him. "Okay. If you want, meet me in the shower in a few minutes."

"Oh, I want to."

I darted from there before my willpower crumbled. I had been avoiding this for the last few days, and it was time to solve it.

Amanda's bedroom door was half open, and I knocked. I could see her sprawled over her bed, still in pajamas, and the faint sound of voices coming from the TV.

I pushed the door all the way open, and Amanda sat up. "What?" she asked, already snappy.

"Can we talk?"

She stared at me for a moment, then shrugged. I walked into the bedroom. It was a mess, with clothes thrown over the chairs, a towel crumpled over the dresser, dirty plates and glasses on the nightstand. She had never been the tidiest person, but this was too far even for her.

I picked up a jacket and a bra from one of the armchairs in front of the window, put them in the other, which was already piled high with clothes, and sat down, facing my sister.

She turned in bed to me, her legs crossed in front of her, and with the remote, she lowered the TV's volume. "What is it?"

"I just ..." I let out a sigh. I didn't want to go around in circles and walk on eggshells with her. To me, honesty was the best move forward. "We were never the best of friends, but we were never this disconnected either. I don't like the way things are between us and I want to know how I can fix it."

She glanced past me, out the window, as if she couldn't even look at me for long.

"It's nothing," she finally said.

"Amanda." I shook my head once. "Are you sure you're the older sister? Because right now, I'm the one who needs to pull on your ear."

She turned her eyes to me, something like anger in them. "Well, you're the ancient witch with the seven-hundred-year-old memories."

I tilted my head. "Is that what is bothering you? That I remember most of my memories and you don't?" I honestly didn't know who else besides Sean and me—and that brief memory I shared with Moira, my mother, and Amanda—would remember anything. They probably wouldn't.

"No!" she snapped.

"Then what is it?"

"It's just—" she clamped her mouth.

"Tell me, damn it!"

"I'm the oldest of us. Until recently, I was the more powerful. But then you turned out to be a freaking queen, the most important and powerful witch of our entire history!"

I gawked at her. "Are you jealous?"

"No!" She looked out the window again. "I'm ... you were my little sister, who would desperately learn from me, try to copy me, and now you're much more than that. You have these big shoes to fill, an incredible destiny, even if dangerous, so much power, and I'm me. Useless and powerless Amanda who needs to hide to not get caught in the crossfire."

My heart squeezed. She was feeling useless while watching her sister become larger than life. That couldn't be easy.

I got up from the chair and sat on the mattress beside her. "You're not useless, Amanda. Not you or mother. Like you said, big things are coming and I'll only be able to get through them with your support, your understanding."

"I'll still be sitting on the sidelines."

I frowned. "Do you want to come train with Anna, Britta, and me tomorrow morning. Maybe we can help you master a spell or two, and you can join the fight."

Her eyes bugged. "Are you serious?"

I couldn't help but smile. "Yes. I would love to have you by my side, but that's only if you can hold your own in a fight. And if you obey whatever we say. If we're in the middle of a bloody fight and I tell you to retreat, you retreat. Deal?"

Tears brimmed in her eyes. "Yes!" She threw herself at me and hugged me tight. I chuckled and hugged her back. "Thank you. It would be amazing to fight by your side and help you make history again."

"We'll see what I'll be able to do."

She pulled back and pouted. "All right, I confess, I'm a little bit jealous too. You're this amazing witch we grew up hearing about. That's still shocking."

I rolled my eyes. "Being me is not as amazing as it sounds."

"You only say that because you're used to it."

"I'm not used to it. I'm only mildly okay with it because I have my memories from the past, otherwise I would be freaking out right now."

She rested her hand on my legs. "Don't freak out. You're powerful beyond dreams, you've got such an amazing legacy, and I bet that whatever you'll do next will be even better."

"Now you're being silly."

"No, I'm not, and you know it." She shot up from bed. "So, when do we start training?"

I smiled. "I just finished a round. This afternoon, we've got a meeting. You can come if you want. If we come back early, we can do your first training session this evening before dinner."

She beamed at me. "Awesome. I'll take a shower now, and I'll be ready to go to this meeting whenever you are." She skipped across the room and disappeared into her bathroom.

I stared after her for a moment, feeling even lighter and better than before. With this issue solved, there was nothing stopping me.

And I could go to the hot man waiting for me.

8

My mother was anxious when we all left to go meet with the other witches late afternoon. I invited her to come too, so she wouldn't feel left out, but the truth was, I didn't want her to come. I loved her to death, but she would only worry me and I already had Amanda with me to do that.

Because we were six now, Shade gave the wheel to Sean and stayed as a cat on my lap. Sean threw a few glances at him lying on my legs. "Don't get too comfortable," he said once, and of course, that only made Shade want to get more comfortable. Soon enough, Sean was pushing Shade to the back where Anna, Britta, and Amanda were.

"You know he was only doing that to provoke you," I said in a faint voice. "The connection between him and me is not like that."

"I know, I know." His voice was still tight. "I remember. Still ... I don't like it."

I hid a smile and turned to look at the road. It had

always been like that. At first, Shade would be mean to Prince Thales, and later when Prince Thales warmed up to him, Shade loooved provoking him. It was a battle of wills, and I was always in the middle.

The meeting place was at a strip mall on the outskirts of New Orleans, where several of the stores were closed and half of the building was empty. We followed the directions and parked our car in the back of the building and entered through the back door. It was dark inside, but when Anna cast a small light bolt to serve as a torch, we found ourselves in a small industrial kitchen.

We continued to a small serving area, and then to the main restaurant, though the chairs and tables had all been piled to the sides. In the front, there was a reception area and a couple of windows that had been covered with leasing posters.

I glanced around as Anna cast more bolts and sent them floating across the place.

Amanda stood by my side. "Are we in the wrong place?"

"No, you're not," came a voice from behind us.

We all turned—Anna, Britta, Shade, Amanda, Sean, and I—ready to fight, but quickly recognized the newcomers: Sadie, Fynn, Moira, Rodd, Clara, Lenora, Penelope, and Marjorie. I hadn't expected to see her here, but I guess with her mother gravely injured, she was the next in line.

Another two Light Order members whom I didn't know stood back, watching.

"Everything okay?" I asked. "How is Queen Denise?"

"The same," Marjorie answered, her voice small. The

last time I had seen her, she had seemed almost vibrant and happy. Now, she looked frail and weak. "Without a miracle, she'll die soon."

"I'm so sorry," I whispered.

She tilted her head. "Are you?"

I frowned. "Excuse me?"

"Are you sorry?" Marjorie asked. "Because we all know who you are. If my mother dies, what will you do? Kill me and take the throne?"

"Marjorie!" Lenora and Fynn snapped at the same time.

I paled. Was she saying I wanted Queen Denise to die? "I don't want the throne," I said, and it was the truth. "I didn't want the throne when I was Arianna either. It happened that I was the one who acted and did something to save us all. When our queen died, the witches turned to me, and suddenly, I was queen." I shook my head. "I never wanted to be one. I hope with all my heart that we find a miracle and Queen Denise recovers, but if she doesn't, you can have the throne."

She narrowed her eyes. "You're lying."

Fynn stepped forward. "Stop it, Marjorie."

"Why? My mother is dying and this one"—she pointed at me —"is coveting her throne!"

"That's enough!" Clara said.

"If she isn't, then those two are planning on taking it for her." Marjorie pointed to Anna and Britta.

"If our queen doesn't want the throne, we won't force it on her," Anna said.

"Our queen," Marjorie repeated through gritted teeth. "My mother is your queen!"

"Technically, we don't belong to the Lightgrove coven." Britta glanced at Anna. "For about six hundred and fifty-ish years now?"

"More, I think," Anna replied, nonchalantly.

Shade glared at them. "You two are not helping," he whispered.

"See?" Marjorie balked. "They're disrespectful! And they are supposed to be the great Anna and Britta—"

Anna stepped forward, her body taught. "What do you mean supposed to be?"

"I said, that's enough!" Clara put herself between Marjorie and us. "Marjorie, you're way out of line." She turned to me and bowed her head. "I'm sorry, Hazel. She's under much stress."

Marjorie shot daggers at Clara's back and then at me.

I didn't know what to say to that. It was clear Clara was dissing Marjorie while treating me like a queen in front of her. That only added fuel to the fire.

"It seems you're all here." Guinevere entered the room from the kitchen. Three other witches I didn't know followed her ... and Laini?

"What are you doing here?" I asked, surprised.

Laini had been in my classes, and she had always been a bitch to me.

"This is my mother, Daisy." She pointed to the witch standing beside her. I didn't remember seeing her before, but I had heard she had been a high-ranked witch inside the Lightgrove coven, with good chances of becoming a council member.

"It's a pleasure to meet you, Queen Arianna." Daisy bowed her head.

I fought a cringe. "Please, call me Hazel." From the corner of my eye, I could see Marjorie seething. "So, you're an Ashmist witch." I frowned. And with her having dibs on the council, that meant that prior to Grace's death, they would have two witches at the top ranks in the Lightgrove coven. The Ashmist witches had been moving some pieces quietly but swiftly. I looked at Laini. "And you too."

They both nodded.

"My great-grandmother had been with the Darkmist long ago," Daisy said. "As she grew up, she realized increasingly she didn't agree with their views and started pulling back. She found out about the Ashmist coven. Back then, they were only a dozen witches and their families, but they helped her flee the Darkmist and welcomed her with arms wide open."

"What was your plan?" I looked at Daisy, Laini, and Guinevere. "Were you spying on the Lightgrove coven? Were you trying to take over?"

Guinevere shifted her weight. "We've tried talking to Queen Denise." She gestured to an older witch beside her. "Laura here even contacted the previous queen and explained the situation to her, but they all shut us out as if we were the scourge."

"It may sound too aggressive, but we wanted to force their hand," Daisy said. "Those of us who could, would infiltrate the Lightgrove coven, and when we had high-ranked witches in their midst, we would create a small mutiny inside the castle and force them to hear us and take us back."

"We know that's not the best way to win their favor," Guinevere said. "But we were desperate."

"If only my mother knew," Marjorie said, venom in her words. "She would have banished you all from the coven long ago." She narrowed her eyes. "And I'm sure she will when she recovers. If she doesn't, then I will." She glanced at me. "I'll comb through the coven until I find all of you."

Guinevere turned to us. "There's none left. When the Light Castle was attacked by the Darkmist and everyone had to flee, we decided it was time to back away. You were already having trouble with the Darkmist. If we added to your problems, you would only resent us."

"There's nothing we can do to change the past," Lenora said, her tone always so serious. "Let's focus on what we can do for the future." She turned to me. "You called us here to talk about a plan."

"It isn't a plan yet, it's more like a wish list," I confessed. "I need your help, all of your help"—I made a point of looking at every witch and Light Order member in the room —"to make it a plan."

"What do you need?" That was Moira. I almost balked at her question. She had never been so prompt and almost nice to me before.

"As it is, the Lightgrove can't fight the Darkmist, especially not in the Light Castle, without help," I said. "So, I asked the Ashmist coven to help us."

"I knew it." Marjorie scoffed. "Absolutely not!"

Lenora turned an icy gaze to her. "You're not queen yet, Marjorie, and you're not a part of the council. You don't decide *shit*."

I gasped, appalled that Lenora had said a curse word like that.

"Lenora is right." Clara nodded. "Please, stay quiet, or we'll need to ask you to leave."

Marjorie stared at them as if they had slapped her. Fynn made a point at glaring at his sister, as if he was warning her he would be the one carrying her out.

Lenora went on, turning our attention to her. "I confess I'm not happy to learn witches who I considered friends were spies." She looked at the Ashmist witches. "But you are right. With our reduced numbers and our queen seriously wounded, we can't take the Darkmist by ourselves. We need help."

"We will accept the Ashmist coven's help," Clara continued. "If they do a blood oath that this isn't a trick and they won't betray us."

Guinevere extended her hand and offered it to Clara. "I'm ready."

Clara and Lenora exchanged a glance.

Clara brought her hand up and traced her index finger on her palm. Blood bloomed from the thin cut. "I promise to welcome the Ashmist witches while they help us defeat the Darkmist witches. My coven and I will treat them with respect and kindness as if they were our own."

Guinevere looked at me, her eyes narrowed. I knew why: Clara had said "while they help us defeat the Darkmist witches." It wasn't the permanent thing she had asked for. But for now, this was all she was going to get. The work to make her wish come true would come later.

I gave her a quick nod.

Guinevere cut her palm with magic. "I promise my coven will be loyal and won't betray the Lightgrove coven while we help them defeat the Darkmist witches."

They grasped hands. A bright light came from within their hands and a buzz of magic coursed through the room.

"It's done," Clara said, lowering her hand. Rodd handed her a handkerchief. "Thank you."

"What now?" Laini asked. I had almost forgotten she was here.

"Now that that is out of the way," I said, "we plan our attack."

***

It took us almost two hours, but we finally agreed on a date, and most importantly, how the attack would go down. There was a lot of shouting, fists clenching, threats, and twice we had to separate witches before a battle began right there.

But now we had a plan, and I couldn't wait to act.

The Ashmists were the first to leave. Next were the Lightgrove, except for Marjorie.

"Can I talk to you?" She glanced at the others. "Alone."

Sean, Shade, Anna, and Britta closed in beside me. Amanda stood like a lost cockroach at the back.

"It's okay," I said, without looking at them. "We'll be fine. Wait for me at the car."

They all hesitated. Sean reached for my hand, gave it a brief squeeze, then left with the others.

When we were alone, Marjorie walked around me, as if measuring my capabilities with her eyes. "What do you want?"

I frowned. I could lie to her, but she was the next one in line for the Lightgrove coven throne. I didn't want to start her reign on the wrong foot.

"I want to stop this mess. I want the Darkmist to back away, the Brotherhood to be extinct, and for witches, light and dark, to coexist in harmony."

She chuckled. "You really think that's possible?"

I tilted my head. "What happened to you? I know we haven't talked much in the Light Castle, but I remember the first time we met. You seemed so light, so happy."

"What happened?" She seemed appalled. "My mother is dying, my coven is falling apart, I'm being forced to make a deal with the enemy, and a queen who was supposed to be long dead is threatening my lineage."

I shook my head. "How many times do I have to say it? I don't want the throne. You can have it. Actually, I hope your mother recovers and she reigns for many years to come."

"You're lying."

I scoffed. "Why would I lie?"

"To trick me. You want me to lower my guard."

"By the light, Marjorie, you're crazy. It doesn't matter what I say, you already made up your mind about me and nothing will change it. I won't waste my breath. Just, please, don't ruin our plan because of your hatred for me. If anything goes wrong, I won't be the only one to go down. We all will."

"We'll see who will ruin what."

I gaped at her. What the hell was she talking about? I shook my head and turned my back to her. "Bye, Marjorie. See you in five days."

"I'm not done talking to you!"

I didn't answer. I walked out of the restaurant.

9

———

FIVE DAYS SEEMED FOREVER TO ATTACK THE DARKMIST AND take the Light Castle back, but it also seemed like not enough time to prepare.

Anna, Britta, and I trained every spare moment. Amanda joined us a few times a day. At first, she could barely cast bolts at the dummies we erected in the back-yard, but within two days, she showed improvement. I could see that she would never be able to go toe to toe with someone like Queen Catarina, but I believed she could at least defend herself long enough to flee to safety.

The sisters found one of my old crystals, imbued with our magic, and gave it to Amanda.

"Have it in your pocket during the battle," Anna told her. "You can draw power from there."

Sean and Shade also trained. Apparently, Shade had learned hand combat and weapons, especially with swords. Sean was rusty at first, but I could see as he remembered more and his new training as a martial artist intertwined with what he knew as Prince Thales, and he got better and better.

Anna and Britta joined their training to see how they would fight against magic, and Sean and Shade held their own. It was a pretty sight to see.

"We need popcorn for this," Amanda said one day while we watched.

I totally agreed.

My mother wandered around the house, fretting about everything. She still held the Lightgrove witches up on a pedestal, especially after finding out that her daughter had founded it, and she was worried about the fight against the Darkmist. If she could, she would probably lock Amanda and me away so we would sit this one out, but I couldn't. This fight was about me. Sometimes, I wished I could keep Amanda out of it, but at the same time, I knew she needed this. I wouldn't take that away from her.

While we prepared, Khalisa called me.

"I have friends to help us, my child," she said.

"You've done enough, Khalisa, and last time your friends helped, I broke the queen's wand."

"We all know the risks of the lives we lead."

"Who are these friends?"

"To be honest, I haven't met them personally yet. The girl, Evelyn, called me a few weeks ago, asking about dragon bones."

I frowned. "Wait. Queen Catarina wore a necklace with a dragon bone. I thought that was fake."

"Oh no, child, that's the real thing. And from what I know, she has a few more. I told Evelyn we're planning on attacking the Darkmist and she's coming to help, as long as she can have the dragon bones."

"Do you trust her?"

"From what I hear, she's like you, child. A light witch born with a dark witch's gift. She faced off with the Nightmist coven in the north, after the dragon bones, and helped save a wolf shifter, a fae, a witch, and a vampire. She and her boyfriend, Asher, are collecting dragon bones and keeping them from falling into the wrong hands." Khalisa paused. "I can't say I trust her completely, but so far, my gut and my magic tell me she's a good person."

"Then I can certainly use her help."

"Great. I'll text you her contact information. You can talk to her about how and where to meet."

I texted Evelyn after I finished the call with Khalisa. She and her boyfriend were driving south from Canada, and they would arrive in time for the battle.

Moira had also contacted some friends, including Almae. Almae couldn't come, but she said she would pass the word around and someone would definitely help us.

My anxiety grew as time passed.

Two days before the battle, the sisters tried lightening the mood by having us sit around the fire pit outside and eat s'mores while drinking wine. Everyone was tense, even Anna and Britta, though they tried to hide it.

My mother barely ate or said anything, and she was the first to go to bed. The others followed suit soon after, and Sean and I stayed alone by the dying fire, snuggled together under a blanket, our wineglasses empty.

Sean nudged me. "Talk to me. What's going through that pretty head?"

I sighed. "You know what. I'm anxious about what's coming, and a little concerned about what will happen after."

"You mean with Queen Denise, Marjorie, and you."

I nodded. "Marjorie seems to think I'm a threat to her, but I don't want the crown. Queen Denise needs to recover." Last I heard, Khalisa had made her some healing potions and she was feeling slightly better.

"You know word about who you are is spreading and some witches will want you to be queen."

"I know, and that scares me. I don't want to cause more problems for the coven. I wish this battle to be over with so we can all move on and live happily ever after."

He kissed the top of my head. "No matter what happens, where we are, as long as you're with me, I'm living my happily ever after."

I turned my face to his. "Are you getting all mushy at me?"

He stared into my eyes, serious. "Hazel, I remembered something from the past. Right before you were ... killed" —his voice strained —"I had talked to my father."

"King Norbert."

He nodded. "Yes. I knew it was going to be a long shot, but I had to try. I asked him to allow me to ask you to marry me."

I stilled. "W-what?"

"After some argument, he said he could see how we complimented each other. He confessed he wasn't a huge fan that you were a witch, but he liked you, he trusted you, so he approved. I commissioned this beautiful ring and I was planning on taking you to our special clearing, and I was going to ask you to marry me. But then ... Hugo betrayed us."

"You were going to ask me to marry you?" I mean, I knew he had loved me, that he loved me now, but I was witch, and he was meant to be the king. I wasn't worthy of his station.

"When you died, it broke me. I thought I wouldn't be able to go a second without you. It was only my quest to bring you back that kept me going. If I didn't have that, I don't know what would have happened to me."

"Oh, Sean."

"I don't want to ever feel like that again. I also don't want anything happen to you again, or to me, and you don't know exactly how I feel about you."

"What ...?"

Sean disentangled himself from me and got down in front of me on one knee. I gasped as he took something out of his pocket and showed it to me. "After you died, I wore it on a chain around my neck." The azure diamond was the center of a flower and smaller white diamonds were the petals around it. Silver metal entwined like vines, forming the ring. "Believe it or not, Anna and Britta kept it after I died. I had it cleaned a couple of days ago, and I even talked to your mother about it." He offered me a lopsided grin. "Though she barely knows me in this life, she approved, so Hazel Rose Levine, will you marry me?"

I stared at him, at the ring, then back at him again.

Tears blurred my vision, and my heart expanded so much, I didn't think it could fit inside my chest anymore.

"Usually, the woman says something at this part," he whispered.

I chuckled. "Yes!" I leaned forward, cupped his face. "Yes, I will marry you." I pressed my lips to his, but before things could get interesting, Sean broke the kiss and placed the ring on my finger. I wiped my eyes and stared at it. "It's so beautiful."

He sat beside me again. "I'm glad you like it."

"I love it." I looked at him. "I love you."

"And I love you."

Sean leaned into me, and I met him halfway. The kiss started slow, soft, loving, but as his hands wrapped around me, and I turned fully to him, straddling him in the seat, our mouths became frantic, as if we couldn't get enough of each other.

With a swift movement, Sean stood, carrying me in his arms, and we barcly broke the kiss as he raced to our bedroom, where we made sweet love.

10

———

EVERYONE KNEW ABOUT THE QUESTION, BUT ME. THAT WAS why they willingly left Sean and me alone by the fire pit last night. So when we woke up early in the morning, they were all waiting for us with breakfast ready in the kitchen.

"Congratulations," they all said with big smiles.

The only one who didn't seem happy was my mother. After we ate, and the sisters insisted they clean everything, I pulled her aside into the living room.

"What's wrong?" I whispered.

A tight smile spread over her lips. "Nothing."

"Don't lie to me."

She glanced at Anna and Britta, who were in the kitchen. Amanda had gone upstairs to change, and Sean and Shade had already gone outside to practice.

"It's ... it's all happening so fast." She looked at me, her eyes somber. "One day, you're my little girl who can barely cast a spell. The next, you're the most powerful witch who ever lived, a war is a day a way, and now you're getting married!"

I lifted my index finger. "I'm not the most powerful witch who ever lived. I was the most powerful witch of the Lightgrove coven seven hundred years ago, and I still haven't recovered my powers." I lifted my middle finger. "It's a battle, not a war." Hopefully, it would all be solved in a day or less. I lifted my ring finger. "People can stay engaged for years. That was a showing of love." And I was pretty damn happy about that.

Her smile relaxed a little. "He does love you. After all of this, you have to tell me how you met him, and how you found out he was Prince Thales."

"That's a date!" I paused. "Don't worry about all of that. We'll take care of everything."

"It'll be hard for me to relax until I know you and your sister are safe. Until then, put up with me."

I hugged her. "It'll be okay."

She patted my back for a second, then gently pushed me away. "All right, now go. I would rather you spend the time you have left before the battle training, not consoling your silly mother."

I smiled. "I will, but if you need to talk, to vent, or even a hug, I'm here, okay?"

She waved me off. "Go, Hazel."

My mother wasn't the most affectionate person. I knew she loved my sister and me fiercely, but she didn't show her feelings easily. This confession had been too much for her.

Smiling, I planted a quick kiss on her cheek, then dashed outside to train.

———————

THE NEXT NIGHT, WE ARRIVED AT JACKSON SQUARE AT midnight. The French Quarter was still in full swing, and even though we were dressed for battle, nobody paid any attention to us.

The day before, Moira had sent us the light witches battle gowns—it was actually a leather vest and pants, and a full-length skirt that opened in the front when we walked. It didn't seem practical, but once I put it on, I couldn't even feel the skirt dragging behind me. She had also sent the Light Order uniform for Sean and Shade ... and for Sean, it had been a captain one, with more embroidery than the others. After all, he had been the founder of the Light Order and its first captain.

Anna and Britta didn't wait for the others to arrive. They started enchanting whoever was here to feel confused and to leave. The sisters approached a coming couple, but after exchanging a few words, they walked away and continued their work in the other direction. I frowned as the couple walked straight to us.

Sean and Shade tensed, and Amanda hid.

"Hazel?" the young woman asked. She was average height, with long, dark hair and dark eyes. She wore leggings, a tee, a leather jacket, and combat boots. She was pretty and I really liked her style. "I'm Evelyn."

"And I'm Ash," the young man said. He was Sean's age and as tall and broad. He also had vibrant blue eyes, though his brown hair was several shades lighter than Sean's.

"Hi." I smiled, suddenly glad they were here. For some reason, I felt like I had a connection with this witch. Like me, she was a light witch born with dark magic. I extended my hand to her. "Nice to meet you."

She lifted an eyebrow. "Should I be shaking hands with Queen Arianna, or should I bow?"

"Please, not you too."

She shrugged and took my hand in hers. "Sorry. Khalisa filled me in on what's going on here. My grandmother was in the Lightgrove coven but moved away for love. She joined a smaller coven later, but everyone always looked up to the Lightgrove, especially to Arianna." She leaned closer and whispered, "You're like a saint."

I chuckled. "Not even close." I gestured to the others. "This is Sean, Shade, and my sister, Amanda. The ones you walked past are Anna and Britta."

Evelyn and Ash stared at Sean and Shade as if they were aliens.

"You both are also legends," Ash said in awe. "Though, no one knew until recently that Arianna's familiar was still alive."

"I've been getting that a lot," Shade said, sounding proud of himself.

"How long have you known Khalisa?" I asked, curious.

"Ash and I have been collecting dragon bones," Evelyn said. "I had heard about a witchdoctor who had great contacts in New Orleans, so one of our stops was here. I felt an immense call from dragon bones here in the city, but when I found out it was coming from the queen of the Darkmist, I moved that to the bottom of my to-do list."

"We couldn't take her on just the two of us," Ash continued. "When you called a couple of days ago, we had recovered dragon bones from the Nightmist coven in the north. We planned on staying up there, but we couldn't pass on this opportunity."

"I'm glad this will also benefit you," I said. "Thanks for coming."

"Thank us after the battle," Evelyn said in a light tone. She looked around. "What can we do for now?"

"You can help us," Anna said from a few feet to our right. "We've sent everyone away from the square. Now, we need to create a ward to keep humans out."

Evelyn nodded. "Got it." She and Ash walked to the sisters.

Movement to my left caught my attention. It was Sadie, Fynn, Rodd, Moira, Guinevere, three Light Order members, and two men I didn't know, walking into the square. With her hands, feet, and mouth magically bound, Robin floated among them.

Moira and Guinevere had set a trap earlier tonight. They spread a rumor that I would visit Khalisa, and of course, Gillian couldn't resist coming after me. Thankfully, she had brought Robin with her again, along with three other witches. The moment they entered Khalisa's shop, the Light Order swarmed the place and kept Gillian and the others occupied while Moira and Guinevere took Robin.

When Robin was away, the Light Order retreated. We could have dealt with Gillian right then, but we needed someone to deliver a message to Queen Catarina.

I frowned. "Are you the warlocks Almae sent?"

One of them nodded. "I'm Aspen." He had long dark dreadlocks, and tattoos covering his naked arms and neck.

"And I'm Boise," the other said. He had shaggy, sandy-blond hair and green eyes. "How can we help?"

This time, Sean spoke. "I only need one of you for this part." Aspen stepped forward. Sean looked at the other men in the group. "The rest of you, come with me. I'll show you where to stand." My heart swelled at seeing him stepping into his old shoes with ease, and thankfully, no one questioned him. Everyone here knew who he was, and I was sure they would follow him blindly anywhere.

As the men went with Sean, Shade glanced at me. I gave him a short nod and he caught up with Sean.

I looked at the witches and warlock before me. "Everything ready?"

Moira nodded. "Yes. We delivered the package." She gestured to Robin, who still floated among us all. "Now we're going to the castle."

"And I'll stay," Sadie said.

I nodded. So far, everything had been going according to our plan.

I turned my attention to Robin. I hated being the villain, but this was the only way of getting her mother. "Comfortable?"

She jerked against the magic holding her afloat, her eyes shooting daggers at me, her words muffled by the magic covering her mouth.

"My guess is that she's not happy," Guinevere said. She frowned. "You've got all you need?"

"Yes." I gestured for Amanda to step closer. "You can go. Send me a message when you're in position, and we'll start."

"All right." Moira looked at Boise. "You're coming with us."

"I know," he answered.

"We'll see you soon," Guinevere said. "Good luck."

"To you too," I said.

Amanda looked at me for a few seconds, then dashed after Moira and Guinevere.

Sadie showed me a tight smile. "This will work out."

"It better," I muttered. I faced Robin again. "Let's do this nicely, okay? Don't fight, don't resist, and no one needs to get hurt."

She yelled, but it sounded more like a faint whine.

A moment later, Anna, Britta, Evelyn, and Ash walked back toward me.

"The square is warded," Britta said. "If a human comes this way, he or she will feel disoriented and changed their minds quickly."

"Good." I looked at my friends, and at the warriors a dozen yards away. Sean and the others seemed to be in position. "Everyone ready?"

"Oh, yes," Evelyn said. "

I smiled, loving her enthusiasm. "Let's get this show started."

11

WE SENT WORD TO QUEEN CATARINA AT ONE IN THE morning. I gave her thirty minutes to come to Jackson Square and duel me, otherwise I would kill her daughter.

To be honest, I probably wouldn't kill her, but Catarina didn't need to know that.

In twenty-nine minutes, Queen Catarina, Gillian, and another two dozen dark witches walked into the square. They took a few steps up then stopped.

"What have you done?" Queen Catarina snarled, her mouth spreading into a tainting grin. Robin, still tied and floating to my right side, jerked at the sight of her mother.

I stood in front of the statue at the square's center. Sadie and Evelyn were on my left, and a little back, were Sean, Shade, Fynn, Rodd, and Ash. The other Light Order members formed a wide half circle around us and the statue.

"Nothing you wouldn't have done. In fact, I think you

would have done much worse." I shrugged. "So, will you duel me? Or are you afraid?"

"Afraid of you?" Her grin spread. "You might have been Arianna, but in this life, you're weak and pathetic." She walked a few steps closer, her witches following her. "I want to know the terms of this duel first."

"If you win, you get your daughter back," I said. "If I win, you leave the Light Castle. You and all of your witches."

She scoffed. "As if I would lose to you."

I shook my head. "Do you accept my terms?"

Her confident, wicked grin faltered for a second. "I do."

I walked three steps in her direction, then halted. Queen Catarina walked up to me, and her witches formed the other half circle around us.

"Perfect," I said.

I lifted a wall between us, encompassing most of the square, and ran. Sadie, Evelyn, and all the others ran too.

"What ...?" Queen Catarina muttered.

The shield fell as fast as it was brought up and a wide circle of runes shone on the ground, trapping Queen Catarina and her witches.

Her face paled. "What have you done?"

I smiled at her. "Tricked you." We had drawn the circle with enchanted chalk after Anna and Britta had put wards around the square. And with magic, we hid it.

"Do you think a mere witches' circle will be able to contain me?" Her voice rose in anger.

"No, I don't, but that should give us plenty of time."

"Time ... for what?" she shrieked.

"Wouldn't you like to know," I teased, feeling powerful, exhilarated.

Aspen came forward and opened a portal for us—warlocks could be so handy—and we all stepped through it, leaving Queen Catarina, Robin, Gillian, and the other dark witches trapped in Jackson Square.

The portal took us to the fake antique store the Lightgrove used as an entrance to the Light Castle, where the others were waiting for us. Even Queen Denise was here.

"Your majesty," I said, reaching for her.

Pale and with shaking arms, she took my hands in hers. "Hazel." She smiled feebly at me. "From the moment I first laid eyes on you, I knew there was something special about you. I could never have imagined how special you truly are."

"I'm Hazel," I said for the tenth time in a handful of days, suddenly feeling like an immature teenager by her side.

"Oh, no, but you're not." She cupped my cheek, and I almost flinched from the coldness of her touch. "You're amazing and you'll save us all."

I frowned. "You shouldn't be here, Queen Denise. You should be hiding and resting."

"That's what I've been telling her all day," Marjorie snapped. She looked like a sour lemon beside her mother.

"That's what we all have been saying since she put this idea in her mind," Lenora said.

"I'm better," the queen said. I knew Khalisa had sent her powerful potions that had come straight from the

Wildthorn and their earthy magic. "I won't get in your way, but I needed to be here."

I could sympathize with that. I looked straight at Marjorie. "I'll be at the front of the battle most of the time. She'll be your responsibility. Keep her safe at all costs, and if that means leaving us behind and fleeing, then so be it."

Marjorie's brows furrowed. "Understood."

"Please, be careful," I said to both. Then, I took stock of the people inside the crowded antique store. "Where's Moira? And Guinevere?"

"They took a dozen witches and are already in," Lenora told me. I stilled. "They saw an opportunity, slipped through the portal, went around the castle, and are now waiting beside a courtyard's entrance. When we give them the word, they will attack from behind while we come from the front."

That was good, actually. "Send them the word in one minute." Then I spoke louder. "Everyone, get ready!"

Beside me, Sean held my hand. "Be careful, my love."

"You too." I stepped into him and rose on tiptoes. He met me halfway and pressed his lips to mine. It was a quick kiss, but full of meaning and love.

He rested his forehead on mine. "Ready to kick some ass?"

I smiled at him. Then, I lifted my hand high. "Ready?" I asked. The room fell silent. "Attack!"

We rushed through the portal and emerged in front of the castle. Two dark witches and a man stood guard. They froze for a brief second upon seeing us, but one of the witches managed to react and throw red sparks up to the sky. If someone saw that, they now knew the castle was being invaded.

Hopefully, even if they knew, they wouldn't have time to react.

We came in like an avalanche. The two witches and the man—probably one of their descendants who made up what they called the Dark Order—went down fast, and in a matter of minutes, we were inside the castle.

More witches and Dark Order members greeted us there. The Light Order and the Ashmist witches engaged them, freeing space for us to pass. Quickly, every inch of the castle we reached became a battlefield.

Our group advanced toward the council room. Whenever someone charged us, we took care of them as fast as we could and continued forward.

Halfway to the council room, we met up with Moira, Guinevere, and their group. They helped us open a path and kept us protected while we focused on our task.

Eight dark witches were inside the council room. Anna, Britta, Evelyn, and Ash battled them while Queen Denise and Marjorie led us to a side wall. There, among two columns, was a hidden door. Marjorie opened it and we shuffled inside.

Magical lights appeared on the wall beside us, illuminating the corridor we were in. The corridor was about three feet wide and seven feet tall and seemed to go on forever.

"This way," Marjorie said, taking the lead. Queen Denise, helped by Clara and Fynn, was right behind her.

As we went, more lights appeared on the walls. We

walked for about three tense minutes until finally the corridor opened up to a small room. There were more corridors sprouting from this room and a staircase in the center.

Marjorie started on the stairs. "Down here."

We all followed her. We climbed down four flights of stairs. By the time we arrived at the landing, Queen Denise was breathing hard. I paused and turned to her, worried.

She waved me off. "I'm fine. Keep going."

I glanced at Marjorie. She sighed but moved on. She led us through another corridor, this one shorter, until finally we stopped at an archway with a heavy wooden door.

She produced a thick bronze key from her pants' side pocket, put it in the keyhole, and muttered an incantation. A wave of visible light magic traveled through the door and a loud click resonated through the corridor.

"In here." She pushed the door open and let me go in first, followed by Sean, and three Light Order members. She got her mother from Clara's and Fynn's arms and went in next. Then, too fast for anyone to react, she dropped her mother, pushed Clara and Fynn back, and closed the door, locking it in place.

"What's going on?" I asked, confused.

On the other side, our friends banged on the door and yelled our names.

Marjorie rested a hand on the door and a magical barrier covered it, muffling all sounds.

Sean and I retreated, and Queen Denise wobbled and fell to her knees.

"Marjorie, what are you doing?" her mother asked.

"Helping you." She reached for her mother and held her hands. She pulled her mother up on trembling legs. "I made a deal with the Brotherhood of Purity, and—"

"You did *what*?" The queen's already pale face became even paler.

"They said that if I deliver Hazel to them along with Arianna's ashes, then they will give me a healing potion that will save you, Mother."

"No," the queen whispered incredulously.

"They said that they will leave us alone." Marjorie stared at me. "Where are the ashes? You said it should be around here, near the heart." She gestured to the center of the room, but there was nothing there.

I opened my mouth, closed it. "Marjorie ... you can't do this. You know they are lying to you."

"They are lying to you," Queen Denise stated.

It was then that the three Light Order members pulled their white hoods off. I gasped and jumped back. Sean pulled out his sword.

Maren stared at me, a vicious grin on his lips. "We meet again."

My gut tightened and I called my magic. "How did you get in?"

"I let them in," Marjorie said. "I gave them the uniform and let them slip in with the rest while you were all busy."

I couldn't believe my ears, my eyes ... "How are you so stupid?"

"Stupid?" she barked. "You're the one who wants to steal our crown and shove us aside. I want you gone!

And this is the way to get rid of you and save my mother."

"You know, they are right." Maren chuckled. "I lied to you."

"W-what?" Marjorie balked.

Maren tsked, as if bored. "It was never my intention to let any of you get out of here alive, and now that I know how to break into the castle, it's a matter of minutes before my brothers are all here and we cleanse this place of witches and their sympathizers."

I reached for my phone, but they lunged at us, and my phone ended up on the floor.

Maren came directly to me, the second Brotherhood member went for Sean, and the third turned to Marjorie and her mother.

I raised a wall between Maren and me. He struck his weapon on it, but with each strike, a painful shock rushed through him.

Suddenly, he changed tactics. Instead of attacking me, he ran toward Marjorie and Queen Denise, who in her weakened state, already had a tough time against that one opponent.

"No!" I cried as Maren aimed at Marjorie.

Queen Denise saw him coming and stepped in the way. His weapon going straight through her heart.

I gasped, my magic slipping from my grasp, my shield breaking.

Marjorie screamed, the sound guttural and piercing. The other man didn't waste time. He struck her too.

They both fell to the ground, blood seeping from their wounds.

Maren and the man turned to me. To my left, Sean whirled under his opponent's arm and brought the pummel of his sword to the man's temple. He fell unconscious.

I didn't have time for this shit. I inhaled deeply, filling myself with my magic, and when Maren's hand was inches from my throat, I let it all out. Dozens of lightning bolts cut through the room, hitting the two men from all sides. After shaking like leaves in the wind, their bodies thudded at my feet.

I turned to Sean. "Are you okay?" I had cast the lightning so it skipped over Sean, Marjorie, Queen Denise, and me. It looked like it was everywhere, but it really hurt the three Brotherhood members.

His jaw worked hard. "Yes. You?"

I nodded and turned my attention to the two women on the floor. Sean and I knelt beside them.

"Queen Denise? Marjorie?" I called.

Marjorie sputtered, her hand pressed to her stomach, her fingers red with seeping blood. Beside her, Queen Denise was immobile, her blood forming a pool underneath her. Sean put two fingers on Queen Denise's throat. A couple of seconds later, he shook his head.

Shit.

"Come on." I hooked my arm behind Marjorie's head. "We need to go."

She groaned and slapped my hand away. "There's no

time. Find your ashes, kill Queen Catarina, and fix my errors."

"Don't talk like that." A sob rose to my throat. I wasn't even that close to either of them, but that didn't mean I wanted to see them gone. "You'll make it."

"I'm not so sure about that, but either way, you need to go," she half-barked, half-coughed.

Sean picked up the bronze key from her pocket and the both of us stood.

"The ashes aren't in here?" he asked, going for the door.

I glanced around. "I don't know." Queen Denise and Marjorie were supposed to take us to where the heart was because I thought my ashes would be hidden with it.

I went to the center of the room, where a round stone on the floor was slightly lighter than the others. I pressed my foot on it. The floor rumbled and a stone pedestal rose from the floor.

"This was where the heart was," I said, confused.

"I moved it," Marjorie croaked. "When the dark witches invaded the castle, I tried stealing it, but there was no time. I took it to the council room. Under the queen's chair, there's a fake bottom. I put it there."

I frowned. "But it was only the heart?"

She nodded. "Only the heart."

That didn't make sense. There should be a pouch with my ashes somewhere.

The loud click of the door unlocking echoed in the room. Sean opened the door, and the others swarmed the room—except for Moira, Guinevere, and Rodd. Where were they?

"Mother!" Fynn shouted. He rushed to the queen. He glanced at Marjorie. "What happened?"

Marjorie's eyes brimmed with tears. "We'll explain later. Now, you all should go. Queen Catarina will be back at any moment, and the Brotherhood of Purity found a way inside."

"What?" Sadie asked, her voice thin.

"I'll take care of them," Fynn said, somber. "The rest of you, go!"

"I'll stay too." Sadie walked up to Marjorie. "Go."

Amanda stood by my side and took my hand in hers. I looked at all of them, my heart broken, but there wasn't much I could do right now.

Without a word, I ran out of the room, Sean glued to my side, and the others right behind us. As we ran, I was told Moira, Guinevere, and Rodd had gone up to either find help, since no one seemed to be able to open the enchanted door, or to join the fight.

We emerged in the council room and Moira, Guinevere, and Rodd fought a bunch of dark witches alongside Anna, Britta, Evelyn, Ash, Aspen, and Boise. They did their best to push them back and keep them from reaching the hidden door.

Lenora and Clara joined them as more dark witches surged in the council room, Amanda went too, but she was clever enough to stay behind them, and Sean and I made our way to the queen's chair in the center of the room.

Sean and I groaned as we tilted the heavy chair and

laid it on the floor. The bottom was one flat wooden slab. I pushed against it, tried to pry it with my nails, Sean used his sword, but it didn't move.

Breathing hard and worried about time, I rested my hand on the wood and tried sensing it with magic. I felt them—the beating heart of the first witch queen and my ashes. They were here, both of them, hidden behind a magical barrier.

Around us, the fight went on and sparks flew over our heads every few seconds. A handful of times, Sean had to step in front of me and deflect the stray bolts with his sword.

Focusing, I placed my other hand on the wood and sent a rush of lightning to its corners. The wood cracked. Eager, I pulled it away and stared at the silk bundle that pulsated in rhythm. I took it in my hands and unwrapped the cloth ... and there it was. The heart of the first Lightmist witch queen.

I blinked and saw the heart in my hands. I was in a dark room that looked like a catacomb, and Prince Thales, Anna, and Britta were with me, along with six members of the newly established Light Order.

"Got it?" Anna asked.

I nodded, still shaking as the heart beat within my palms.

"Then let's go before Jewell arrives," Britta urged.

I wrapped the heart into a blue velvet cloth and put it inside a small bag I had brought for this. Then, we ran out of this place, seconds before it was swarmed with dark witches.

A scream echoed through the room, and I snapped

back to reality. A few yards to my left, Clara fell to the floor, her hand over her chest. Oh, no, not another one.

"Hazel, focus," Sean said, firm and yet gentle.

"Right." I wrapped the heart back into the silk and set it down. We would put it back on the pedestal later and place some powerful wards around it, so no one could steal it. I looked at the now empty compartment under the chair.

Where were my ashes?

Like I had done before, I closed my eyes, called my magic, and trusted it. I placed both hands under the chair. A rush of magic swept over me and suddenly, I felt a small weight in my hands.

I gasped and opened my eyes.

A small blue velvet pouch lay in my hands.

I looked up at Sean and we both smiled.

A tingling coursed under my skin, and I knew what to do. I stood, opened the pouch, and handed it to Sean. He sprinkled the ashes over my head, and to my amazement, the ashes glittered as they fell around me.

Before reaching the floor, the ashes twirled around my legs, my waist, my arms, my head.

I inhaled deeply and suddenly it was all there. My magic, my memories, everything.

I stared at Sean and knew he had his full memories back too.

When I looked to the battle, most of the witches had stopped, and were watching us in amazement.

This was my opportunity to use who I was, who I used

to be, the legend I had become, and stop this nonsense fight.

"My fellow witches—"

A loud laughter echoed through the room as Queen Catarina walked in, followed by Robin, Gillian, and another wave of dark witches.

"Great show, Hazel," Catarina said.

The fight around the room sizzled and the witches and men took their sides.

"Glad you're enjoying it," I said, coming to the front of the line.

"It's time to end this," she snarled. "You owe me a duel."

My turn to show her a lopsided grin. "My pleasure." I sent lightning directly to her chest. She barely had time to move out of the way, and hit another of her witches in the chest. The witch convulsed and fell unconscious—I hadn't hit to kill, but to numb.

With an enraged cry, Catarina came to me and the both of us battled. I threw my lightning at her; she threw her dark magic at me. Her bat flew at my face, trying to distract me, but Shade, in his cat form, jumped from the side, caught the bat in his mouth, and killed the damn thing.

Catarina cried again and renewed the strength behind her attacks.

For a moment, everyone stood still, watching us. Until Sean yelled and lunged at the nearest Dark Order warrior. Chaos descended upon the room.

Shade smartly went after the other witches' familiars.

He had the advantage of shifting into and out of his human form, and in less than five minutes, he had killed three more.

To my surprise, Catarina was stronger than I thought but I was stronger than her.

I sent a lightning bolt that hit her stomach and made her fall to her knees in pain. Approaching her, I brought up a pillar made of lightning, trapping her in a circular prison.

"Yield," I said.

She laughed through the pain. "Never."

"Yield, or I'll make you regret you ever existed."

She rose to her feet and glared at me. "I haven't even started." She wrapped a hand around the dragon bone hanging from her neck and channeled its power.

Evelyn stepped forward, her arm raised. The dragon bone shook in a battle of wills. A few seconds later, it snapped from its chain and flew directly into Evelyn's hand.

"What ...?" Catarina was at a loss for words.

"My affinity is to control dragon magic, accessed via their bones," Evelyn explained as she pocketed the bone.

"You have nothing now," I told Catarina. "You can't fight me. Yield."

She lifted her chin. "Do your worst."

I twirled my hand and the pillars arched inward. They struck her, shaking her body as if they were frying her. Catarina crumpled to the floor, unconscious.

Something in me darkened. I should kill her. I should rid the world of her evilness, but I couldn't bring myself to do it. I had killed before, but I really didn't want to do it again. If I could win this battle without killing, I would try.

"Enough!" I shouted. Slowly, the battle died out around me. "Lightgrove and Ashmist witches, apprehend the Darkmist witches." Some dark witches resisted, but they had seen their queen at my feet. Most surrendered, but some fled the room as if they would be able to leave the castle. "Queen Catarina isn't dead. She'll be taken to—"

Murmurs started and rose fast.

I turned around and saw Catarina lunge at me, a black magic bolt in her hand, aimed directly at my heart.

Swiftly, Sean stepped between us and buried his sword in Catarina's chest. The bolt in her hand blinked away. With wide eyes, she looked at the sword and the blood pooling around the blade.

Sean withdrew the sword and Catarina folded to the floor.

"Mother!" Robin yelled. She ran to the queen. Sean tried to attack her too, but I held his arm and shook my head.

Robin leaned over her mother and cried.

"It shouldn't have been like that," I said, my voice low. I cleared my throat. "I'll be clear. Any witch who tries something like that again, at me or anyone else, will be dealt with." I made a point of turning around, staring at the dark witches who were now subdue. "Your fate isn't decided yet, but know that as light witches, we'll be honorable, as long as you are too."

While turning, I assessed the damage in the room. There were a few bodies here and there, including

Marjorie's resting along the wall beside the hidden door. Her eyes were open and unseeing. My chest constricted.

"Hail to the queen!" someone yelled from the back.

"Hail to the queen!" a few more said.

Suddenly, the whole room chanted, "Hail to the queen," as they knelt and bowed their heads. Sean gave me a knowing smile, then joined them.

I stared at them, confused but proud.

I had wished to make the Lightgrove a safe place again. This wasn't how I wanted to make it happen, but it seemed to be the only way.

A Light Order member appeared at the door. "Help!" he yelled, then he halted, looking around at the scene.

Sean stood. "What is it?"

"T-the Brotherhood of Purity are invading the castle," the man said.

"Light Order warriors, we have another battle." He glanced at me, winked, and then rushed out of the room. The Light Order warriors followed him, and Shade, Ash, Boise, and Aspen went with them.

12

This wasn't exactly what I had wished for, but in some ways, it was even better.

Sean and I stood on the ballroom's dais, with the council members beside us. I wore an elegant white and silver gown and a new, light white crown on my head.

Sean was handsome in a modern take of his old blue uniform, a silver sword hanging from his waist. He didn't have a crown yet, because we didn't want to rush the wedding, but soon enough, he would have one, and he would be called king.

He would probably be the first King of the Light Order, but hell, as its founder, he could do whatever he wanted.

He picked up one of my hands, brought it to his lips, and gave it a soft peck. He knew how nervous I was about this, how unworthy I felt. The only thing holding me together right now was the fact that I knew he and the council had my back. They wouldn't let me falter.

I turned to the ballroom and smiled at the hundreds of

faces staring back at us. It was now hard to imagine that only a week ago, this castle had been the site of a bloody battle that changed the entire course of the Lightgrove coven.

After the battle, the Light Order dealt with the Brotherhood of Purity who invaded the castle. If they hadn't wiped out the entire New Orleans sector, it would have been close.

While they fought, we rounded up the dark witches and gave them a choice: live in prison or join us. They were warned, though, that if they stepped out of line, there would be heavy consequences. Two of them screamed bloody murder and tried to attack me; they were killed on the spot. A handful stayed quiet and were taken to the prison underneath the castle, and the rest were willing to try.

Then we helped the wounded and took care of the dead. In the battle, Moira and Lenora had been badly hurt, but our healers said they would be okay. Others had minor injuries like scrapes and scratches that needed to be cleaned and would be fine.

And we lost some people too. Queen Denise, Marjorie, Daisy, two other Ashmist witches, one of the Light Order captains, and three warriors.

When dawn came, we gathered the dead in the backyard, had a small ceremony for them, and burned their bodies.

After, I was called into the now clean council room with Lenora, Clara, Guinevere, Moira, Fynn, Anna, Britta, and Sean.

"We need to appoint a new queen and assign new members to the council," Lenora started the meeting.

I knew where this was going, and a wave of unease filled me. "I don't think—"

"It's unanimous," Clara said. "If you accept, you'll be appointed queen and Sean will be the new High Captain of the Light Order."

My stomach clenched. "I—"

"As for the council, I'm suggesting we take Anna, Britta, Moira, and Guinevere as new members," Lenora continued.

I frowned. "Wait. Guinevere is Ashmist. Does this mean you'll let them join us permanently?"

"I thought that was what you wished," Lenora said.

I almost smiled as I looked at Guinevere. She seemed happy. "Yes. Yes, it is."

"Anyone else you would like to add to the council?" Clara asked.

I shook my head. In my opinion, Anna, Britta, and Moira were great choices. I didn't know much about Guinevere yet, but we needed someone to represent the Ashmist witches on the council, at least until they felt like they really belonged to the Lightgrove coven.

"Then it's settled," Lenora said. "The coronation will be in one week."

And that was the end of it. Fast and quick. If I had objected, I was sure they would have found a way to go around it.

The applause reverberated in my ears, bringing me back to the present. In front of the crowd were my mother and Amanda, both of them with tears in their eyes. Shade was with them, looking as smug as usual.

To their left were Sadie, Fynn, Rodd, Evelyn, and Ash. To their right were Khalisa, Boise, Aspen, and Almae, who had come for the ceremony.

Behind there were Laini, Mei, Cleo, along with Penelope and the other initiates—Belinda and a couple of others had died during the Darkmist's first invasion. And behind them were all the other witches—the old and the new ones. The Light Order was spread throughout the room, though a dozen of them were on duty and stood guard.

"Long live the queen!" Rodd yelled. Everyone joined him.

I felt a mix of pride and introversion. One side of me wanted to enjoy this, the other side wanted to hide behind Sean.

After the coronation, Sean and I walked around the ballroom, greeting everyone, hearing congratulations over and over, and also a thank you here and there.

Most people looked at us as if we were gods. That would take some getting used to.

My mother dissolved into tears when Sean and I stopped by her, Amanda, and Shade. "My beloved daughter, queen of the Lightgrove coven," she said between sobs. "Someone pinch me."

Amanda rolled her eyes. "She always had been a fan, now it's worse," she muttered.

Next, we greeted Khalisa.

"I'm so proud of you, child." She embraced me tightly. "I know you'll do amazing things."

"Thank you." I pulled back and looked at her. "And please, let Queen Yira know I didn't forget about her wand. Now that I have my full power, I should be able to figure out a way to fix it."

When Sean and I turned from Khalisa, we faced Almae, Boise, and Aspen.

"Thank you for coming, Almae," I said. "And for sending help when we needed."

"No worries, my dear." She took my hands in hers and held them tight. "If only I had known when I first examined you, maybe I could have seen hints of it. Alas, it wasn't supposed to be."

"Everything worked out in the end," Sean said.

Almae smiled at him. "That, it did."

We thanked Boise and Aspen again, before moving on to Evelyn and Ash.

"Thank you for calling us," Evelyn said.

"That was all on Khalisa," I said. "But I'm glad she did." I tilted my head. "You know, you could stay."

"Both of you," Sean added. "We could always use another Light Order warrior."

"The offer is tempting," Evelyn said. "But I can sense too many dragon bones out there that are being used for nefarious reasons. I would rather find them and keep them safe."

I nodded. "Well, if you ever find them all, or decide to retire, know you're welcome here."

"That means a lot," Ash said.

Next was Moira, Rodd, Fynn, and Sadie. Moira had come down the dais from her council position, and Sean had made sure to take Fynn and Rodd off duty tonight.

"You've surprised me," Moira admitted. "In a good way."

My brows rose. "I thought you hated me, even when you were helping me."

She grunted. "Don't push it."

I smiled. Having her on the council beside me would be fun.

"Thank you to the three of you," I said to Sadie, Fynn, and Rodd. "You helped me and Sean when no one seemed to be on our side. That meant a lot." Beside me, Sean nodded.

"It was our pleasure," Sadie said.

It was a shame Sadie was considered too young to be on the council, though she was a little older than I was, otherwise I would have invited her too.

"You can count on us for anything," Rodd said, his eyes on me. Beside me, I felt Sean tense. As I expected, Sean had found out Rodd had asked me out before, and since then, things had been a little awkward between them.

With time, I was sure they wouldn't only respect each other but turn out to be great friends.

Then it was Guinevere's turn. Since Grace had died, Guinevere had been the leader of the Ashmist coven, but now the coven had been absorbed into the Lightgrove.

"Thank you for keeping your word," Guinevere said. "We're all excited about the future."

"Me too."

After her, Sean and I greeted a few more of the new witches, some initiates, and the rest of the coven.

Finally, after we greeted and talked to everyone, the party really started. One of the Light Order members' hobby was DJing, so he was in charge of the music. The center of the ballroom became a dance floor, and food and drinks weaved among the guests on enchanted trays. Despite the ugly scene from last week, everyone seemed to be enjoying the party.

When the DJ played a slower song, the dance floor filled with couples.

Sean, who had his arm around my waist or at the small of my back all evening, extended his hand to me. "May I have this dance, Your Majesty?"

I rolled my eyes at him. "Do not start with the 'your majesty' thing." I slipped my hand in his and he took me to the center of the ballroom.

One corner of his lips tugged up. "Why not? You are the queen."

"Between you and me, I'm just Hazel. The girl with the dyed hair, the piercings, the tattoos, leggings, leather jacket, and combat boots." Dressing up in a gown and fancy clothes was nice, but sometimes I missed my old self.

I had redone the red streak in my hair, my piercings and tattoos were still apparent, but for some reason, I felt like they were hidden. From me and everyone else.

"I love all sides of you," he said, his tone serious. He wrapped one arm around my waist, took my hand in his, and started moving us around the dance floor. "The rebel side, the worried side, the committed side, the loyal side, and also the queen side."

My cheeks warmed up. "I love you too, you soft-hearted future king." He chuckled, then quickly lost the smile. "What is it?"

"Just ... I have been thinking a lot about my parents. How am I going to lead this life and still keep them a part of it."

I frowned. He had already mentioned this subject earlier this week. I had suggested telling his parents the truth, but Sean said they would probably freak out, think we were nuts, and either commit Sean to an asylum, or cut ties completely.

"We'll find a way," I told him. "Even if we have to pretend to work in the French Quarter's antique store and visit them often."

He tilted his head. "Which reminds me, you haven't met them in this life yet, have you? We should go spend a weekend with them."

I smiled at him. "I like that idea." It would involve a lot of moving pieces. The council wouldn't let me go without a dozen witches and another dozen Light Order warriors, but we would find a way to make it work. "We should plan to go in two weeks."

Sean made the math in his head. "That's Christmas. Perfect!"

I looked at him and my heart squeezed, my chest flooding with love. I leaned into him, and he met me halfway, pressing his warm lips to mine for a quick kiss.

I glanced around. My family and my friends were here,

the Lightgrove had expanded and welcomed witches in need, and I felt like I had finally found my calling.

How had I been so lucky? In my previous life, and in this one.

I leaned against Sean and rested my cheek on his collarbone. "This, right here, is perfect."

He kissed the top of my head. "I agree."

HAZEL AND SEAN'S STORY MIGHT BE OVER, BUT THERE ARE many more books in the RITE WORLD for you. Have you read them all? Check it out here: https://www.juliana haygert.com/books/rite-world-reading-order/

BONUS: want to read an exclusive scene from Sean's POV? Download it here!

To read a special and exclusive book about another light witch, join my Facebook Group and find the book called *The Light Witch* to download on the "featured" tab!

who finds out she's a demon hunter, and the half-demon intent on protecting her against all evil.

The Vampire Heir (Rite World 1: Rite of the Vampire): a dark and mysterious paranormal romance about a vampire and a young woman with a secret.

The Warlock Lord (Rite World 4: Rite of the Warlock): a thrilling and kick-ass paranormal romance about a were-wolf and warlock.

The Wolf Forsaken (Rite World 7: Rite of the Wolf): a heat-wrenching tale about a lost wolf shifter and a fae princess on the run.

Heart Seeker (The Fire Heart Chronicles book 1): an urban fantasy series about a young woman who finds herself at the center of a mysterious supernatural world.

Destiny Gift (The Everlast Series book 1): a post-apocalyptic urban fantasy series about a young woman with a special power that can save the world.

Don't forget to sign up for my Newsletter to find out about new releases, cover reveals, giveaways, and more!

If you want to see exclusive teasers, help me decide on covers, read excerpts, talk about books, etc, join my reader group on Facebook: Juliana's Club!

ABOUT THE AUTHOR

While USA Today Bestselling Author Juliana Haygert dreams of being Wonder Woman, Buffy, or a blood elf shadow priest, she settles for the less exciting—but equally gratifying—life as a wife, a mother, and an author. She resides in North Carolina and spends her days writing about kick-ass heroines and the heroes who drive them crazy.

Subscribe to her mailing list to receive emails of announcement, events, and other fun stuff related to her writing and her books: www.bit.ly/JuHNL

For more information:
www.julianahaygert.com

facebook.com/julianahaygert

twitter.com/julianahaygert

instagram.com/juliana.haygert

goodreads.com/juliana_haygert

pinterest.com/julianahaygert

bookbub.com/authors/juliana-haygert

youtube.com/julianahaygert

tiktok.com/@julianahaygert

ALSO BY JULIANA HAYGERT

To find links and more info, go to:
www.julianahaygert.com/books/

Shorts
Into the Darkest Fire

Standalones
Daughter of Darkness

Rite World: Night Wolves
The Night Calling (Book 1)
The Night Burning (Book 2)
The Night Hunting (Book 3)
The Night Rising (Book 4)

Rite World: Vampire Wars
The Darkest Vampire (Book 1)
The Darkest Witch (Book 2)
The Darkest Magic (Book 3)

Rite World: Lightgrove Witches
The Midnight Test (Book 1)
The Midnight Spell (Book 2)
The Midnight Flame (Book 3)
The Midnight Secret (Book 4)
The Midnight Hunt (Book 5)
The Midnight Wish (book 6)

Rite World: Blackthorn Hunters Academy
The Demon Kiss (Book 1)

The Hunter Secret (Book 2)
The Soul Bond (Book 3)
The Shadow Trials (Book 4)
The Infernal Curse (Book 5)

Rite World
The Vampire Heir (Book 1)
The Witch Queen (Book 2)
The Immortal Vow (Book 3)
The Warlock Lord (Book 4)
The Wolf Consort (Book 5)
The Crystal Rose (Book 6)
The Wolf Forsaken (Book 7)
The Fae Bound (Book 8)
The Blood Pact (Book 9)

The Wyth Courts
Winter King (Book 1)
Spring Warrior (Book 2)
Summer Prince (Book 3)
Autumn Rebel (Book 4)

The Fire Heart Chronicles
Heart Seeker (Book 1)
Flame Caster (Book 2)
Earth Shaker (Book 2.5)
Sorrow Bringer (Book 3)
Soul Wanderer (Book 4)
Fate Summoner (Book 5)
War Maiden (Book 6)

The Everlast Series
Destiny Gift (Book 1)
Soul Oath (Book 2)
Cup of Life (Book 3)
Everlasting Circle (Book 4)

<u>*Willow Harbor Series*</u>
Hunter's Revenge (Book 3)
Siren's Song (Book 5)

<u>*Breaking Series*</u>
Breaking Free (Book 1)
Breaking Away (Book 2)
Breaking Through (Book 3)
Breaking Down (Book 4)

www.ingramcontent.com/pod-product-compliance
Lightning Source LLC
Chambersburg PA
CBHW061925220726
48287CB00018B/1019